Holly Jolly Christmas

A Seeking Justice Christmas Novella

"Get rid of all bitterness, rage and anger, brawling and slander, along with every form of malice. Be kind and compassionate to one another, forgiving each other, just as in Christ God forgave you." - **Ephesians 4:31-32**

Books by C.C. Warrens

Then

Rain flowed down the truck's windshield in rivulets, causing the gray street ahead to ripple. Gus squinted, straining to see the edges of the road.

If he'd known a storm was brewing, he might've waited 'til morning to run to the store. But his pregnant wife had a hankering for chocolate icing, and they were short on sugar.

The store was only a jaunt down the road, and if not for the rain, he would've been home by now. Martha was probably pacing the kitchen in her slippers, butter and eggs already in the mixing bowl.

Where was the drive up to the house? He had to be close. He rubbed the sleeve of his shirt over the window to clear the fog stretching across the glass.

The road had to be there.

"Couldn't have just disappeared."

The headlights glinted off something white in the middle of the road, and as the wiper passed over the windshield, Gus caught one heart-stopping glimpse of a little girl.

He slammed on the breaks so hard that it should've driven the petal through the floorboard, but the truck skated across the water on the road, propelling him toward the child.

1
Now

Marx sat in his car, staring at the familiar white house a hundred feet away. Somehow, after all these years, it was still standing—like a wraith in the darkness. The painted siding was faded and chipped, and the porch roof leaned like an old man with a hunched back.

Strange how the painful memories of his childhood remained crisp and strong even as the house and the man who inflicted them withered with age.

Dad's favorite excuse still echoed in the back of his mind—*this is for your own good, Richard.* As if that single sentence could justify the beatings that left a little boy sobbing into his Teddy Bear for hours.

His fingers gripped the steering wheel tightly as he wrestled with the desire to shift the car into reverse and back out of the driveway.

He'd made the trip from New York City to his hometown in Georgia many times, but he hadn't set foot in this house since the day he walked out almost thirty years ago.

His hand fell to the gear shift, and he started to roll out of the gravel drive toward the street, but then he glanced at the petite young woman curled up, asleep, in the passenger's seat of his car. She was the reason for this trip.

Her life had been ripped apart more than once by the darkness of this world, and there was nothing Marx could do to erase those awful memories, but he could try to smother them with beautiful ones.

He wanted her to experience family in a way that she hadn't since she was a little girl, and he knew his mother would welcome her with loving arms. If he had to play nice with his father for that to be possible, then he would.

With a heavy breath, he put the car in park and turned it off. He looked over at his sleeping passenger. She had been an anxious wreck for most of the trip, her claustrophobia making confined spaces nearly unbearable, and he'd been relieved when she finally fell asleep.

"Sweetheart."

She let out a soft moan before snuggling deeper into the jacket he had draped over her after she dozed off.

He smiled and brushed a strand of hair from her face. "Holly."

She inhaled a slow breath through her nose and stretched like a cat waking from a nap before her eyelids cracked open. Not too long ago, waking up to a man beside her would've made her freeze in fear, but now she blinked groggily, completely relaxed. "Time for a break?"

"Time to get out. We're here." Her small foot peeked out from beneath his jacket—clad in candy cane-striped socks—and he reached into the backseat to grab her shoes. "Here."

She shrugged off the extra jacket and rubbed the sleep from her eyes with the heels of her hands. "I don't see a hotel."

"You can't see anythin' with your hands in your eyeballs."

"Ha-ha." She snatched her boots from him. "Where are we? I thought we were staying at a hotel."

"We are. The hotel's about ten minutes away, but I thought we'd stop by my parents' house for a quick visit."

If things went as badly as he expected, they would head to the hotel for the night and start the drive back to New York City tomorrow morning.

"You're worried about how things are gonna go with your dad, aren't you?"

Either Holly was picking up his ability to read micro expressions or he hadn't masked his thoughts well enough. "And you accuse me of bein' a mind reader?"

A soft smile touched her lips. "Don't dodge the question."

"I might be a little worried." He and Dad hadn't parted on good terms, and the time and distance apart had done nothing to ease the pain and anger between them. "He's never been very fond of me."

There were times when Dad seemed to love him, but those brief moments were scattered across years.

Holly leaned over and hugged his arm. "I'm fond of you."

Her love and affection was a rare gift that few people received, and he was grateful to be one of them. He kissed the top of her head. "I'm fond of you too, sweet pea. Now get your shoes on."

She wiggled her feet into her boots and pulled her fluffy hat down over her head before braving the chilly night air.

The thumping music from the neighbor's backyard grew louder as Marx got out of the car and closed his door. When he lived here, an elderly couple had owned the house next door, but he supposed they had passed on long ago.

Out of the corner of his vision, he noticed Holly bobbing up and down on her toes. "What's the matter with you?"

She bit her bottom lip before reluctantly admitting, "I have to pee."

Marx snorted in amusement. "About time. After a large sweet tea and two chocolate milks, I'm surprised you weren't doin' that dance an hour ago."

"I was asleep an hour a . . . wow." The Christmas lights wrapped around the porch railing of his family's home glittered in her widened eyes. The lighted garland

and candles brightening every window gave the house a warm and inviting appearance, even if it was only warm and inviting from a distance. "It's so pretty."

What most people took for granted, Holly appreciated with a childlike wonder that Marx had lost long ago. It amazed him that she had managed to hold onto it despite all she had been through.

Her excitement gradually gave way to uncertainty. "Are you sure your family won't mind me being here for Christmas?"

"Mama's gonna love you."

His dad, on the other hand, might have a hernia when they appeared on his doorstep. It would've been polite to call ahead, but that would've hemmed him in, preventing any excuse to turn back and head home.

A subtle but familiar shift in Holly's body language tripped the alarm in the back of his mind, and he tracked her frozen gaze to the sparse patch of trees to their left. He didn't see anything unusual about the shadowy property line between his parents' yard and the neighbor's, but he knew better than to ignore Holly's instincts.

Someone was there, someone he couldn't see, and after the events of this past year, he was suspicious of anyone who lurked in the shadows. His hand dropped to the gun on his hip when a man staggered out of the trees and across the uneven lawn.

He looked young—late teens, probably—and Marx doubted the bottle he tipped to his lips was filled with root beer. The bottle must have been empty because he shook it before carelessly tossing it aside. It hit the ground a few feet away and shattered into a dozen glittering pieces.

Marx stepped closer to Holly to shield her from anything else that might come flying their way. Her eyes remained glued to the boy as he tripped over something, pitched forward, and faceplanted in the damp grass, but Marx's nearness seemed to relieve some of her fear.

When the boy finally fumbled back to his feet, he kicked at the ground in anger, as if the overgrown blades of grass were to blame for his lack of coordination, then lurched behind the nearest tree.

His ignorant, inconsiderate behavior pricked Marx's temper. This was his mama's home; no one had the right to throw trash on the lawn or wander over and relieve themselves on her property.

They were going to have words, but first he wanted Holly somewhere safe and well lit so he could keep an eye on her. "Come on, sweetheart."

He wrapped a hand gently around her arm and led her to the porch. She didn't put up a fight, but he knew her stubbornness would make an appearance the moment he tried to leave her there.

"I'm gonna go talk to the neighbors." Anxiety flowed over her features, and he rubbed her arms through her jacket. "You'll be safe here on the porch."

Her attention darted to the tree where the man had retreated. "What if he's violent? What if he has a gun and he tries to hurt you?"

He should've known that her concern was for him and not herself. "I'm a cop, remember? I can take care of myself."

She gave him an incredulous look that pointedly reminded him of all the times he'd been injured or nearly killed. "I wanna—"

"You're not comin' with me."

"But I can—"

He held up a hand to cut off her argument, and she bristled like a ticked off kitten—adorable ferocity that terrified no one. "We're not arguin' about this. And don't you follow me."

She glared at him, and he realized that commanding her to stay had been a mistake. She would follow him out of sheer stubbornness now. Unless he explained *why* he didn't want her coming with him.

He prayed for the right words. "I know nothin' about these people, Holly—who they are, how dangerous they are, or how many of them there are. But I do know that drunk men don't often remember their manners when it comes to pretty girls."

Her face paled and she swallowed hard as the meaning behind his careful phrasing registered. The fear in her eyes made him wish he could take the words back, but he needed her to understand why she couldn't follow him.

He wasn't concerned that someone would physically attack her—he would level any man who tried to touch her without her permission—but after what she had been through, no one *needed* to touch her to cause her pain.

Her foster brother had left her with a minefield of physical and emotional triggers; a raised voice, a threatening posture, even a suggestive comment could send her spiraling into a panic attack. He wanted to protect her from that.

He kissed her forehead in apology. "I'll be right back."

When he started across the grass to speak with the neighbors, she didn't try to follow. The fear that his words dredged up left her feet rooted to the porch.

2

Now

Martha swung her ample hips to the Christmas song pouring from the nearby speakers as she pressed her cookie cutter into the sheet of dough on the counter, creating the last wreath that would soon be frosted and showered with green sprinkles.

She placed it on the tray with the others and slid them into the oven, bumping the oven door shut with a hip. She might be in her early seventies, but age couldn't steal the joy that was ingrained in her old bones.

She just finished setting the timer when, out of the corner of her eye, she noticed the Christmas lights on the front porch dim.

Some Grinch had ripped down her decorations a week ago, and she had to piece them back together and replace the broken bulbs. As she stared at the window alongside the front door, she saw the lights blink again.

"Interestin'."

The lights weren't flickering or shorting out; it was like someone was walking back and forth across the porch in front of them.

Who would be on her porch at this hour? She wasn't expecting anybody until Christmas day.

The passing thought that it might be one of those boys dropping by to stir up more trouble made her want to grab her cast iron skillet and march out there to teach them a thing or two about consequences.

But Jesus didn't go bashing people over the head with skillets, so she couldn't very well do it either.

Lord, forgive me for my violent thoughts.

She pulled the tray back out of the oven so the cookies didn't burn and turned off the timer. Scooping a few cookies from the cooling rack onto a plate for her unexpected visitor, she started down the hall.

She glanced at Gus as she passed the living room. He was a difficult soul—she wanted to thump him over the head with a rolling pin more often than she wanted to hug him—but he was *her* difficult soul, and she loved him.

He was slouched in his worn recliner, mouth agape as he snored, a half-eaten sandwich in one hand. Martha shook her head. That man could fall asleep on the toilet.

She peered through the window beside the front door and was surprised to see a tiny, red-haired girl pacing back and forth on her porch in purple rain boots.

The girl's hair was woven into loose braids that framed a pale, cherubic face, and she wore a large fluffy hat that kept slipping down over her eyes.

She would push it back up and then rub her gloved hands together as though she was cold. It was nearly forty-two degrees, and she was wearing a hat,

12

gloves, and a puffy green coat that made her look like a walking stuffed pepper. "What in the world?" Martha muttered to herself.

The girl looked vaguely familiar, but she didn't know anybody as fine-boned and pale-complected as this girl. She would fry like an egg on pavement in the Georgia sun. Though there seemed to be more clouds than sunshine these days.

The inner door let out a rusty creak when Martha opened it, and the girl jumped, bumping into the potted pine tree beside her and knocking it over.

"Easy," Martha said, pushing open the screen door so she could step outside. She glanced at the little tree she would need to re-pot, then back at her unexpected guest. "What can I do for you, baby?"

"Um,"—the girl glanced over her shoulder into the yard—"I'm just waiting."

Martha's eyebrows lifted. "This ain't the bus stop, honey. If you're waitin' here on my porch, it'd be polite for you to tell me why."

"Oh, um . . . he told me to stay here because there was a man in the yard. One of the neighbors."

Martha wanted to know who *he* was, but at the moment she was more concerned with one of those boys being in her yard. They were nothing but trouble. And she certainly couldn't leave this girl out here alone at night with them wandering about, regardless of who she was or who she was waiting for.

"It's not safe for you to be out here alone. Come on and wait inside."

The girl hesitated at the offer. "I'd rather wait out here. In case he needs me."

Martha sighed. She couldn't force the girl into the safety of her home, but leaving her alone outside wasn't an option either. She would never forgive herself if something bad happened to her.

"All right. But you're at least gonna have a cookie." She held the plate within her reach. "In fact, why don't you take three. You look half-starved."

The girl lit up, but she reached out to grab a cookie with a cautious manner at odds with her excitement. "Thanks." She took a nibble and then eyed the remaining cookies.

"Go on."

At Martha's behest, she snatched two more cookies with quick fingers and stashed them in the bag draped across her narrow shoulders.

Martha puzzled over her as she set the plate of cookies aside. There was something about the girl's eyes—the color of burnt honey, with shadows as deep and dark as the Mississippi—that pulled at Martha's heart.

Something awful had happened to this girl, a pain beyond words, and Martha wanted to wrap her in her arms and tell her everything would be all right. "Are you okay, honey?"

The girl nodded.

Martha pressed her lips together as she studied her. She looked so familiar, but she just couldn't place her. "Where you from?"

"New York City."

"Oh how nice! I been thinkin' about takin' a trip there. My baby boy is a big-time detective in the city, and he's . . ."

The pieces came together in Martha's mind—the pale, cherubic face, the red hair, the city—and she pressed a hand to her chest.

The girl looked familiar because Martha had a picture of her on her kitchen prayer board. It was a blurry black and white photo she had printed out at the library, but she was certain it was the same girl. It *had* to be.

"You're my boy's Holly, aren't you?"

"Yes, ma'am."

"Oh, baby, I been waitin' to meet you!" Martha pulled her into a hug so suddenly that Holly choked on the crumbles of cookie in her mouth. "Oh goodness." Martha released her and patted her on the back. "Swallow the cookie, honey; don't inhale it."

After Holly finally got her coughing fit under control, she cleared her throat and said a little hoarsely, "I thought he would've told you we were coming."

"Must've slipped his mind. But I am so happy you're here, honey."

Doubt flashed through Holly's eyes, but it was the cautious hope in her voice that nearly broke Martha's heart. "Really? You don't mind me being here?"

15

"Mind?" Martha pulled her into another hug, giving her a squeeze. "I wouldn't have it any other way!"

She didn't know much about this girl's history—her boy, Ritchie, was frugal with details—but the fear of being unwanted was written all over her face. She couldn't imagine how somebody could look at her and then send her on her way. Before today, Martha had never spoken to her or laid eyes on her, but she had prayed for this sweet child every day for the past nine months. And she loved her already.

Somethin' wrong with people, Lord.

She ran a hand over one of Holly's red braids, her fingers brushing the purple ribbon tied into a bow at the bottom. "You're welcome here anytime. And by anytime I mean I have a spare room upstairs that's all yours."

Holly laughed. "Thanks."

"Now, where's that boy of mine? I taught him better than to leave a young lady standin' by herself in the dark." When Holly turned toward the neighbor's house, Martha's gaze followed. "Those boys are no good. You keep away from them, you hear?"

A line of concern appeared between Holly's eyebrows. "But Marx is over there. Is he gonna be okay? Are they . . ."

The blaring rap music abruptly died, leaving a split second of deafening silence before male voices rose in protest. Something wasn't right, and Martha had a bad feeling in the pit of her stomach. "I'd feel better if you were safe inside, away from whatever they're on about over there."

Holly walked to the edge of the porch, her attention fixed on the escalating dispute beyond the trees. The bonfire roaring in the yard next door cast bits of moving shadows, but nothing that helped her see what was happening. Holly shifted restlessly, visibly struggling to remain on the porch.

"Put that down!" Ritchie shouted, his furious voice cutting through the others, and Holly hopped down the steps and dashed into the darkness.

"Holly, come back!"

What was the foolish girl thinking?

Probably the same thing you're thinkin'. Her gaze landed on the decorative wooden sled leaning against the side of the house. If those troublemakers tried to hurt her boy, she'd give them all a good whack.

She picked up the sled and started down the steps when a feminine yelp drew her up short.

Oh Lord, don't You let nothin' happen to my babies.

A distorted shape—much too large to be Holly—strode across the lawn, heading straight for the porch. Martha lifted the sled, prepared to defend herself, when the Christmas lights illuminated the features of the man: tall and lean with graying hair at his temples, and vibrant green eyes so like her own. The fear and fight drained out of her and she dropped the sled back to the porch floor. "Oh, Ritchie!" Her baby boy was home.

And he was carrying a squirming, protesting Holly by the waist. "Put me down!"

Ritchie set her feet on the porch and released her, his expression hard. "I told you not to follow me."

Holly crossed her arms indignantly. "I thought you were in trouble. I was gonna help."

"How exactly were you gonna help me with four drunken idiots?" He lifted a challenging eyebrow, and Holly shifted her feet before giving a reluctant shrug. "Exactly. You run headlong into trouble without a plan, and that's what gets people hurt. And don't give me that 'I was plannin' on makin' a plan' line."

Holly let out a huff, and Ritchie pinned her with a look Martha recognized, one she'd given him more than once when he was a bullheaded boy. "Don't you huff at me, young lady. I'm just tryin' to keep you safe."

Martha rested a hand on top of Holly's head. "Seems to me that's what she was tryin' to do for you. Just 'cause she's tiny don't mean she ain't mighty."

Holly perked up at her words, and Ritchie sighed. "Don't encourage her, Mama. She gets herself into enough trouble."

She smiled and opened her arms. "Come give your mama a hug."

3

Now

Marx hugged Mama tightly. It had been nine months since he last saw her, and that was far too long between visits. A shouting match with the neighbors wasn't the way he'd intended to announce his arrival, but it could've been worse.

One of the kids sitting around the bonfire had chucked a bottle at his head when he unplugged the speakers, and another one had squared up for a fight. Marx showed the kid his badge and gun and suggested he think twice. He might not have any authority in Georgia, but a badge and gun still carried weight.

Holly came crashing through the trees just as the boys were dispersing, and he scooped her up before she could rile them back up. She meant well, but she was more distracting than helpful.

Marx kissed Mama's cheek and drew back, studying her. She looked as though she'd aged *years* over the past several months—her once dark hair had turned completely silver, and the creases around her eyes had deepened.

Something was wrong, and his gut instinct told him it had something to do with the neighbors. He tipped his head in their direction. "When did they move in?"

"Couple three months back. You remember the elderly couple who used to live there—the Martins? Jenny passed away several years ago, and her husband was moved to a nursin' home. The house was passed down to their grandson, Alex." She grimaced. "Hard to believe they share the same blood."

Their grandson had been running around the yard in diapers the last time Marx saw him, which made him thirty one, maybe thirty two. None of the kids sitting around the fire tonight could've been older than twenty one, and some were certainly younger. "He a foster parent?"

"You might think so with all the kids spendin' time there, but no. They're just neighborhood kids."

"And they're causin' problems by the looks of things."

Mama's lips pinched. She didn't believe in speaking ill of folks, which was why Marx made it a statement rather than a question. Her refusal to comment only confirmed his suspicions.

"She told me to stay away from them."

Marx's gaze dropped to Holly, who was staring at the neighboring house with twitchy discomfort. She had come a long way from the skittish girl he found sitting on a curb, but unfamiliar men still made her nervous. He plopped a hand on her head and her oversized hat fell down over her face. "You'd be wise to heed the warnin'."

She ducked out from under his hand and threw him a disgruntled glare as she fixed her hat. "Stop that."

"Where are your belongin's?" Mama frowned at the absence of bags and suitcases on the porch. "Don't tell me you came all this way but forgot your luggage."

"No, we didn't forget. The suitcases are in the car." Where they were going to stay until they reached the hotel.

"Well go get 'em then. They ain't gonna carry themselves up to the bedrooms."

"We're just droppin' by for a quick visit, Mama. We're not stayin'."

"Don't be ridiculous. We got perfectly good beds upstairs and plenty of food to eat. Though I haven't had much time to prepare for guests."

A reluctant smile crept across Marx's lips. Mama didn't need notice to *prepare* for guests; she was always prepared. "You know the beds aren't the issue, Mama."

She waved off his concern. "I won't have my boy stayin' in some expensive hotel when his home is right down the street. You and your daddy are just gonna have to get along."

"We have a reservation."

"That's fine. I'll cancel it for ya while you go get your things. And don't forget to lock your car doors. Neighborhood ain't what it used to be." She held out an

21

arm to Holly. "Let's go get you settled into a room for the night."

They left him alone on the porch, confused and frustrated. Despite hotel reservations and rehearsed excuses, he was in exactly the position he'd planned to avoid. He could navigate his way through an interrogation with a serial killer without breaking a sweat, but somehow, Mama always managed to outmaneuver him.

His eyes roved over the place that had been his home for the first eighteen years of his life. The walls crawled with memories, some treasured, and some that reminded him of why he left.

He used to sock-skate on the slippery hallway floor and slide all the way to home plate in the kitchen. He cracked his head on the table more than once, but he was up and sliding again before the knot finished swelling.

The cupboard under the kitchen sink became his secret hideout when Dad was looking to teach him another lesson:

Dad's voice boomed off the walls like thunder. "Don't you hide from me, boy!"

The familiar smack of the belt against Dad's palm made him tremble, and he curled into a tight ball beneath the kitchen sink, arms wrapped around his knees.

"You're only makin' this worse for yourself!"

He listened to the slow creak of his dad's footsteps on the floorboards and tried to burrow deeper into the corner. The cupboard door flew open and a hand reached in, grabbing a fistful of his shirt and dragging him, screaming and crying, from the safety of the cupboard.

The click and whoosh of a belt sliding from the waistband of Dad's pants was a sound he would never forget. The beatings had been painful, but the pain of never measuring up had lingered long after the welts and bruises faded.

The quiet groan of floorboards drew his attention to the man who stepped into the living room archway. The large and intimidating figure his dad had once been had shriveled into a stooped, wrinkled old man.

"Richard."

Marx didn't miss the lack of warmth and respect in his tone or the contempt shining in his eyes, and he returned it in kind. "Dad."

"I see you invited yourself for the holidays." He eyed the suitcases Marx was holding before looking toward the top of the steps. "And you brought your mistress."

"Holly's not my mistress, and if you listened half as much as you *judged*, you would already know that."

Dad made a phlegmy sound of disbelief in the back of his throat. "And I suppose she's not livin' with you neither."

Holly *was* living with him, but not for the reasons his father believed. "My livin' arrangements are none of your business."

"I raised you better. Even if you're not sleepin' with the girl, which I seriously doubt, need I remind you that you're supposed to be avoidin' the *appearance* of evil?"

Marx dropped the luggage with an angry thump. "Don't preach at me, old man. There is nothin' you have to say that I wanna hear."

"I won't have disrespect or sin under my roof!"

"Then I guess you better move out!"

His dad's face reddened, and he opened his mouth to snap a reply, but a meek voice from upstairs interrupted. "Marx?"

Holly stood at the top of the steps, her body language guarded. Marx made a conscious effort to suppress his anger before speaking. "What is it, sweetheart?"

"Your mom asked if you want your old room or the spare room across the hall from mine."

"This isn't his home anymore. He gave that up when he chose to run off like a coward."

That tiny but mighty ferocity Mama had mentioned sparked to life in Holly's eyes. She was fiercely protective of the people she chose to let through her walls.

Dad's shoulders tensed, and the wild anger that used to deform his face just before he lashed out with violence crawled over his features. "Don't you look at me like that, girl."

Holly stared him down, unflinching. "He's not a coward. A coward is a father who abuses his family instead of protecting them."

Dad stepped back as if she'd slapped him across the face, the shock of her verbal backhand diffusing his anger.

"I know what you did. And maybe you should think twice before throwing around words like *coward*."

Marx forced a calmness into his voice that he didn't feel. "Why don't you give us a minute, sweetheart. And you can tell Mama my old room is fine."

Holly was still visibly wrestling with her own anger when she turned and stalked back down the hall.

"I will tell you this once." Marx leveled a warning glare at his dad. "I don't care how angry you get, you don't touch her. Ever. And if you have a problem with me, that's fine, but don't you dare make Holly pay for it. She's been through more than enough."

He picked up his luggage and started up the stairs. He could feel Dad's eyes boring into his back with every step, and he gritted his teeth.

Lord, for my mama's sake and Holly's, please help me not to lose my temper.

It was strange how being back in his childhood home, in Dad's presence, could undo all the progress he had made in his faith. He was supposed to embrace people with love and forgiveness, and yet he felt anything *but* the love of Jesus for that man, and he didn't see it changing any time soon.

4

Now

Entering his old bedroom was like stepping back in time. Mama had kept everything dusted and organized the way he liked it—a few model cars lined up on the hanging shelf, car magazines stacked on the dresser, and his baseball glove at the foot of the bed.

He realized with a pang of regret that she must have come up here to clean regularly in the hopes that someday he would come home.

As he picked up the old baseball glove, a memory took shape in his mind:

The ball soared across the sky toward him, and the smell of new leather filled his nostrils as he raised his glove to snag it out of the air. He was going to catch it this time.

The ball slapped his unbroken mitt and bounced out, rolling through the grass back to Dad's feet. He swallowed hard and his legs wobbled as he braced himself for the explosion.

But Dad plucked the ball from the grass, turned it over in his hand, and smiled. "Takes time to break in a glove. Come on. Let's try again."

They tossed the ball and chased wild throws until the sun sank behind the trees. And in all that time, he only caught it once.

Marx pondered the memory as he set the glove back on the bed. The memories he had taken with him from this house were of an angry, scripture-spouting, drunk, not of a man who played ball with him when he was still too small to reach the upper cupboards in the kitchen.

He wasn't sure what to make of that memory.

He left his luggage and crossed the hall to the guest room where Holly would be staying. He found her seated on the edge of the bed with Mama, a stuffed bear with more patches than a quilt in her hands.

"And he took it with him everywhere," Mama said.

Marx lifted an eyebrow at the bear that had somehow managed to survive his mud slogging, tree climbing, creek-swimming childhood. It was the stuffed animal equivalent of a cockroach—immortal.

Mama looked up at him with a sparkle of treasured memories in her eyes. "You remember this bear?"

"Mmm hmm." He took the stuffed animal from Holly, turning it over in his hands. His initials were stitched into the bottom of the bear's left foot: RDM. "His name was Blue Bear."

Holly cocked her head curiously. "But he's brown."

"I was four. I had a limited vocabulary." When she tried to mimic his Southern *mmm hmm*, he bonked her on the head with the bear and she giggled. "How is this thing still in one piece?"

Mama lifted her chin proudly. "Tender love and care. I stitched that bag of fluff back together more times than I can count."

"I remember how mad you were when I ripped his left leg off and deemed him an amputee."

"You made him a crutch out of a stick until I could sew his leg back on."

Marx laughed and handed the bear back to Holly. When he was a kid, new toys were rare; either they took care of the ones they had, or they had nothing.

Mama patted Holly's leg and stood. "I'll let you two get comfortable." She kissed Marx's cheek. "So good to have you home, Ritchie."

"Ritchie?" Holly mouthed silently once they were alone. Marx narrowed his eyes—only Mama was allowed to use that nickname—but Holly only smiled, mischief glinting in her eyes.

Marx laid her suitcase on the bed and sat down beside her. "You gonna be all right here?"

She shrugged. "Are you?"

"I'll manage." He leaned his elbows on his knees and stared at the floorboards, contemplating how to approach the discussion about Dad's behavior. "About what happened downstairs with my dad . . ."

She drew her feet up onto the bed and hugged her knees. "I'm sorry if I made things worse. It just makes me so angry that he treated you that way."

"I'm not mad at you. I appreciate you wantin' to defend me, but my dad is . . ."

"Kind of scary." Her tone suggested she found him more than *kind of* scary, but she had a knack for understatement. "But I know you won't let him hurt me."

He'd hoped she hadn't recognized the threat of violence in his dad's face, but of course she had. Given her history with men, her survival had been contingent on recognizing the warning signs.

As far as Marx knew, Dad had never hurt a woman—in fact he always insisted that they be treated with respect—but Holly wouldn't have the benefit of his father's love to protect her from his temper.

"If you don't feel safe around him, if he does anythin' to make you feel threatened or uncomfortable, I need to know. And we'll leave, all right?"

She nodded. "Why do I get the feeling he hated me before I even walked through the door?"

"He's aware of our livin' arrangement, and he doesn't think it's possible for an unrelated man and woman to live together without there bein' a sexual relationship."

"But you told him, right? That we're just . . . that you're kind of, you know, like a . . . a dad."

Her words warmed his heart. He had told her before that he loved her like a daughter, and although he knew she regarded him as a father-figure, it was the first time she'd ever said it. He wrapped an arm around her and pulled her close enough that he could kiss the top of her head.

Holly could brighten anyone's day if she put her mind to it, but it was love and affection that made her glow bright enough to light up an entire room. She tipped her head back to offer him a small smile that radiated joy.

"I tried explainin' it the last time I was down this way, and I'm sure Mama tried too, but he's always been quick to think the worst of me."

"Well . . . his opinion's stupid."

"Eloquently put."

She grinned at his sarcasm and gave him a playful shove. "Maybe this trip will be a good thing for you and your dad. Help you guys work some things out."

He appreciated her hopeful attitude, but he doubted there would ever be anything good between him and Dad.

"You sure you got everythin' you need in here?" He tapped her suitcase, which had to be the lightest suitcase a woman had ever packed. "I can run down the street to the store if you need anythin'."

"I think I'm good."

She unzipped a compartment of her suitcase and pulled out an inexpensive picture frame. It couldn't have cost more than a couple of dollars, but it preserved the only picture she had of her family, and she held it as if it were the most precious thing in the world.

She ran a gentle finger over her twin sister's face and a sad smile crossed her lips. He could see the fond memories and the heartbreak colliding behind her eyes like a thunderstorm. She'd been nine years old the last time she saw any of them alive.

If there had been anything left of her childhood home, he would've taken her there for Christmas, but there was nothing except cobwebbed walls and the fragments of a life that could've been.

It reminded him that life was fleeting and fragile, and one day all he would have left of his family were pictures, memories, and a soul-deep longing for just one more moment with them.

"You look like your mama," he said, tucking a curtain of red hair behind her ear. "Except your ears. You got your daddy's ears."

She flashed him a scowl and pulled the hair loose, letting it fall back down to cover her ear. There were only two things Holly hated about her body—her height, which usually made her the shortest adult in the room, and her ears, which were just a bit too big for her head. He thought it was cute the way they popped out.

She placed the picture frame on the nightstand before he could point out any more similarities, and after a second of consideration, moved the electric Christmas candle from the window next to it.

She plopped back down beside him. "I have a question."

"All right."

She snatched the Teddy bear up by one skinny leg and showed him the initials on the bottom of the foot. "What's your middle name?"

"I'm not tellin'."

"That's not fair. You know mine."

"Yes I do, but I'm not tellin' you my middle name. It's a secret."

She puckered her lips to one side, calculating, and he knew she was going to spend the next several days trying to unravel the mystery of his middle name.

"I'm gonna go downstairs and catch up with Mama. If you need me—"

"Call you or come get you, I know."

"Right. And remember that you're—"

"Never an inconvenience." They may have had this conversation a few dozen times.

He lifted his eyebrows. "And you're always complainin' about *me* interruptin' *you*. Won't even let me finish a sentence."

"I let you finish that one."

He chuckled. "Goodnight, Peanut."

The nickname earned him another scowl. "I'm not a peanut."

He smiled and ruffled her hair. "Sleep well." As he left the room, she was already settling into the bed with her journal and a snack bag of mini marshmallows.

He closed the door and started down the hall, but he paused at the top of the steps when his dad's irate voice carried from the kitchen. "I don't want them here."

Mama challenged his frustration with calm reason. "It ain't just about what you want, Augustus. I barely seen my baby at all these past thirty years. I will not let you push him away again."

"I didn't push him away. He left."

"'Cause you was too hard on him!"

Marx sat down on the top step, the familiarity of this moment tugging him back into the body of that little boy forty years ago. He used to creep out of his room at night and sit down on the steps to listen to his parents argue. He never dared make a sound, but he hoped with every fiber of his being that this would be the last time, that Mama would finally throw Dad out and lock the door.

But the arguments always went the same: Mama pitched a fit about Dad's drinking and behavior, Dad roared incoherently back, and Mama sighed before walking away.

Her voice brought Marx back to the present. "I never should've let you raise him that way, but I was too young and too naïve to know better until it was too late."

"I raised him the way a boy should be raised! I did everythin' I could to teach him respect and how to be a man."

"You taught him fear!" Mama shouted. "And I will not have that in this house. Not anymore."

"And I will not have their sin in this house! Look at that girl he brought here. Tell me he's livin' with a girl that looks like that and he's not—"

"A girl that looks like what?" There was a moment of outraged silence before Mama demanded, "Looks like what, Augustus?"

Marx knew where this conversation was headed. Holly was a beautiful girl, and despite the fact that she wore no makeup and dressed to conceal her body, men noticed her. Even when she wore that ridiculous hat that swallowed her head.

Dad let out a guttural noise somewhere between a scoff and an irritated pigmy goat. "You know exactly what I mean. Girls like her ain't nothin' but trouble."

"Just 'cause she's young and pretty don't mean she's trouble. You need to give her the benefit of the doubt, and you need to tell our son the truth. Maybe it'll do you both some good."

Something slapped the table top—probably Dad's hand—and the old man stormed by and out the front door in a cloud of anger.

Marx tapped his fingers on his knees as he stared at the front door. What truth was Mama talking about? He already knew Dad was an alcoholic and a philanderer. What more was there to be ashamed of?

The steps creaked and groaned as he stood and started down them. He'd hated those steps growing up; there was no sneaking up or down them, and they had given away his late nights more than once.

He hadn't snuck out often, but there were a few young ladies who, on occasion, tempted him to risk the consequences. The first time he slipped out to meet a girl, he was thirteen, and little Amy Williams had given him his first kiss.

That peck on the lips had left his face on fire and his tongue tied in knots. He'd wanted more—what teenage boy didn't—but Amy only gave him a coy smile before flitting away into the night.

Amy had been his first love. Shannon had been his last, and he supposed that was how things would stay.

When he walked into the kitchen, Mama was sitting at the table, massaging her temples. She smudged her fingers beneath her eyes in an effort to disguise her tears, but it did nothing to alleviate the redness around the edges.

Marx opened the fridge, giving her time to compose herself, and was surprised to find the shelves on the door lined with coke cans rather than beer bottles. Maybe Mama had finally broken down and gotten Dad his own mini fridge for his addiction.

He grabbed a can and walked back to the table, pulling up a chair beside Mama. "Dad still drinkin'?"

"No. He stopped a while after his last heart attack. Doctor's orders. It was a long and rocky road, and it liked to killed the both of us, but he's been sober for six months."

Marx popped the tab on his Coke. "Six months?" He couldn't recall Dad being sober for more than a day. He lived in a cycle of hungover meanness and drunken fury. As a child, Marx hated him for that, but as a man, he wondered what Dad had been trying to hide from. "Was Dad always . . . the way he is?"

"I s'pose he's always been a little short-fused, but when we met, he was funny, bright, full of hope. And he was drop-dead gorgeous. Just like my boy." She patted his cheek, and Marx smiled. "We was happy, so happy. For a while. But then . . . things changed."

"Changed how? Why?"

"It ain't my place to tell you why. All I can say is that some things happened, as they do in life, and they changed your father. He became a different man."

Marx didn't like the sound of that. He'd met too many women who entered into marriage only to discover that their husbands had a dark side. "Did he ever hurt you?"

Surely he would've seen it, but then, knowing Mama, she would've done everything possible to make sure he didn't.

"Goodness no, nothin' like that. But he . . . did make life difficult, and there was times when I asked God why He gave me such a fool of a husband."

"Why didn't you leave him?" He wished she would've packed their bags in the middle of the night and driven them across the country, some place his father wouldn't find them.

"There were nights I thought on it, but I love your father, Ritchie, despite all his flaws. And I made a promise to the Lord—for better or worse. Just happens there's been a lot of worse."

Marx twisted the tab on his Coke until it snapped off, and then tossed it on the table, furious with himself. He should've been here for her, but he'd only been thinking about himself when he left. He joined the army, hoping it would take him far away from this place.

"You hungry?" Mama asked, dragging him from his thoughts. "I'll fix you a snack. How about a meatloaf sandwich?" She didn't wait for his answer before getting up from the table.

"That's not exactly a snack, Mama. Don't you have any yogurt or crackers?"

She blinked at him as if he had just asked for a stalk of celery to gnaw on. "You used to love my meatloaf."

"I do, but—"

"Good, I'll cut you a nice thick slice." She went to work preparing his snack, and he didn't bother arguing any further. Mama was going to make him the sandwich whether he wanted it or not. "That Holly is the cutest little thing," she said, slathering a slice of bread with mayonnaise. "Thin as chicken wire though."

Eight months ago, Marx would've agreed, but Holly had come a long way. She was almost back to her normal weight. "Believe it or not, that's about as big as she gets."

Mama grunted, as if he had just issued a challenge. In his family, *healthy* meant a few extra inches of biscuits and pie around the waistline, something Holly lacked.

"You're too skinny, too. Don't they have food in New York City? I'm gonna have to come up there and stock your cupboards. Make sure you're eatin' proper."

"I have to stay fit for my job, Mama. Mashed potatoes and fried chicken every day aren't gonna do me any favors when I'm chasin' down a suspect."

She clicked her tongue. "Hogwash. You put a little fat on you and all you gotta do is sit on him. Your suspect ain't goin' nowhere then."

Marx laughed. How did she expect him to *catch* his suspect? Roll down a hill in pursuit? With his luck, he'd roll right over the guy and then get charged with excessive force.

She brought his sandwich over and set the plate in front of him, along with a glass of sweet tea. "I was thinkin' maybe tomorrow that I might make some cookies for Holly. Does she have a favorite?"

"Holly likes just about anythin' that has sugar in it." Marx took a bite of his sandwich and the combination of flavors melted over his tongue. No place in New York City could capture the taste of homemade Southern food.

"Maybe I'll let her help me make 'em."

"That might be the last you see of your kitchen for all the smoke her cookin' causes."

"Oh, she can't be that bad."

"Oh, yes she can. I'm thinkin' about gettin' her one of those Easy Bake ovens for children so she can bake things without causin' a fire or settin' off the smoke alarm in my kitchen." He took a bite, then paused with

39

the hunk of sandwich in his cheek. "Don't tell her I said that."

"Don't talk with your mouth full." She tapped her fingers on the table, her expression thoughtful. "Holly seems like a very sweet girl. I can see it, like God wove her heart into every part of her bein'—her eyes, her smile, the gentleness of her voice, that sweet way she giggles. But her pain . . . I can see that, too." She looked at him, and the bite of meatloaf in his mouth became harder to swallow. "What happened to her, Ritchie? Who hurt that baby?"

He set down the sandwich, all desire for food gone. The things Holly's foster brother had done to her were too difficult to put into words. "You don't need to know the details, Mama."

"You told me a man took her, but you never said . . ."

He reached over and took her hand, giving it a gentle squeeze. "She'll be okay, Mama."

Holly might still be picking up the pieces of her life, but she had come a long way from the shattered shell of a girl she'd been after the abduction.

Moisture blurred the vivid green of Mama's eyes. "I won't pry, but is there anythin' I need to know? Anythin' . . . I should keep in mind while she's stayin' here?"

Marx released her hand and sat back in his chair as he thought about it. "Sometimes she has panic attacks. Usually I can help her through them, but not always.

She's very cautious around men, and every now and then she has night terrors."

"You mean nightmares?"

"Worse. Sometimes the dreams are so bad that she wakes up terrified and disoriented. If that happens, it's best if you and Dad keep your distance."

The look on her face mirrored the anguish in his heart, and even though she needed to know, he regretted telling her. She was too compassionate. He stood and wrapped his arms around her from behind as her silent tears became quiet sobs, her heart breaking for a girl she barely knew.

5

Now

Holly poked her head out of the guestroom into the dark hallway. It was a little before three in the morning, and the house was silent.

She wrapped her sweater around herself, tucked her feet into her slippers, and stepped out into the corridor. Curiosity drew her gaze to Marx's closed bedroom door. He was probably more uncomfortable staying here than she was, and she entertained the thought of whispering through his door to see if he was awake.

The idea popped out of existence when a roaring snore from down the hall sent her heart rate tripping. There was the human Buzzsaw that had kept her awake all night. Unfamiliar, startling sounds in a new place did not make for a restful sleep.

She had already written in her journal, read a few passages in her Bible, paced the length of her room, and now it was time to wander.

She walked softly down the hall toward the staircase. The banister was wrapped in white lights and pine garland, with silver and red plaid bows. She rubbed the little bows between her fingers. They weren't soft and silky; they were more of a coarse burlap material.

Her plans to find the kitchen and grab a glass of water changed when she reached the bottom of the steps. She felt like a snoop, but they had gotten here so late that no one had shown her around the house.

She padded into the living room, drawn by the leftover scent of a fire in the fireplace and the aroma of fresh pine. A beautiful Christmas tree stood in the living room, waiting to be decorated with the boxes of ornaments surrounding it.

Holly leaned in to smell the branches. She'd never had the extra money for Christmas trees during the ten years she was on the run, and she always missed them during the holidays. This one, with its soft needles, reminded her of home.

Trees with firmer needles held the weight of the ornaments better, but they were too prickly, so her family had always chosen soft needles. This one was smaller than the ones her family used to cut down. Or maybe it was because she was bigger now. Still, she doubted she could reach . . .

She stretched up onto her toes, then dropped her heels back to the floor. Nope, couldn't reach the top of it. Would Ms. Martha let her help decorate it? She tried not to get her hopes up, just in case she said no.

Holly resumed her wandering adventure around the bottom floor until she found herself in the kitchen. Paper wreaths and cardboard carolers hung from the cupboard doors, and there was a metal Christmas tree on the counter, each one of its six branches curling into hooks at the ends. But instead of ornaments hanging from the ends of the branches, there were dainty snowflake glasses.

They were beautiful. And probably breakable, so she didn't touch them.

She spotted a snowman candy jar sitting there on the counter like an open invitation. She gravitated toward it and bent down, admiring all the colorful homemade candies.

How to choose . . .

She plucked off the snowman's hat and stuck her hand into the jar, grabbing the first candy she touched. She pulled out a little black blob dusted with powdered sugar and popped it into her mouth.

The flavor spread across her tongue and she scrunched her nose in disgust. She spat the candy into the trash and tried to wipe the flavor off her tongue.

"Licorice. Yuck."

Maybe picking a piece of candy called for a bit more strategy. She dove in for a second piece. Pink and red were usually safe. She pulled out a red piece and sniffed it.

Cinnamon.

"I hate cinnamon."

The third piece she pulled out was pink and cherry flavored. Perfect. Cherry was her favorite. She sucked on the delectable candy while she perused the kitchen.

She stopped in front of a corkboard that was covered in pictures and Bible verses. She didn't expect to recognize any of the faces, but then she found a grainy black and white photo of herself.

When had it been taken, and why did Ms. Martha have it?

She removed the tack and took the picture down for a closer look. A Bible verse was penned in the white space to the left of her photo:

Do not fear, for I am with you; do not be dismayed, for I am your God. I will strengthen you and help you; I will uphold you with my righteous right hand.

She read the verse three times, letting the words sink into her soul. Sometimes it was easy to forget that God was not overwhelmed by the things that overwhelmed her.

When she felt like the world might shake her apart, He held her together. And when fear of what lay ahead left her frozen in place, He took her hand and led her forward, whispering into her heart, *I am with you.*

And He was. He was with her now as she fought to rebuild her life, just as He'd been with her then, when evil was fighting to tear it apart.

The certainty that He was with her was all that kept her from curling into a ball whenever she thought about those awful days, and about the man who had left her with nothing but the hope that her next breath would be her last. But it hadn't been her last, and she was still standing.

She started to place the picture back on the corkboard when a movement outside of the kitchen window drew her attention. She looked toward it and found herself staring directly into a face on the other side of the glass.

6

Now

A shrill scream ripped Marx out of a fitful sleep, and he bolted upright in bed, flinging aside the blankets. It took his tired brain an extra second to identify his surroundings—his childhood bedroom—and then he rushed across the hall.

He expected to find Holly in the throes of one of her night terrors, but the guestroom door was open and her bed was empty.

"Holly?"

He checked the other guestroom and the bathroom. Both empty. That meant she must be downstairs, and her frightened scream had nothing to do with a nightmare.

Terrifying possibilities pounded through his mind as he went back for his gun, a new one springing up with each quickening beat of his heart. As a detective, he had seen the evil and depravity mankind was capable of, and he hoped there was nothing more than a burglar in his family's home.

As he turned the corner, he collided with Holly, who was scampering blindly up the steps. She let out a yelp, and he caught her arm to keep her from tumbling all the way back to the bottom. "What happened? What's the matter?"

She pointed toward the kitchen. "A face. In the window."

He descended a few steps to see the window over the sink, but the glow of the electric candle sitting on the frame distorted his view of the outside. Having a light in the window provided prowlers with a detailed view of everyone and everything inside.

"What the devil is goin' on down here?" Dad appeared at the top of the steps, annoyance stamped across his features.

"Holly saw a face in the kitchen window."

Dad's hunched shoulders snapped straight, and he looked toward the kitchen, searching for a threat. The only movement in the kitchen was the artificial flicker of the candle flame. He grunted dismissively. "Probably just saw her reflection."

Marx narrowed his eyes at the suggestion that Holly was too stupid to know the difference. "Think what you want. I'm gonna check it out."

The idea of a prowler made him uneasy. Too many serial killers and sexual predators started out by peeping in windows.

Dad's jowls quivered with indignation and he stomped down the steps past them in his slippers. "It's my house. If there's a problem, I'll handle it."

He wrenched open the closet built into the underside of the stairs and disappeared inside. Marx shook his head and returned his attention to Holly. "I need you to stay put, sweetheart. I don't want you endin' up on the wrong side of a gun. And if you hear or see anythin' suspicious, just call out, okay?"

She nodded and plopped down on the steps, seeming to take his instructions to "stay put" literally.

Marx made his way down to the foyer and slipped his feet into a pair of Dad's old boots, which fit perfectly. Dad closed the closet door hard, emphasizing his dissatisfaction.

"I don't need your help."

Marx ignored his father's door-slamming tantrum and peeled aside the curtains covering the window by the door. "I don't care what you need. While Mama lives here, and while Holly's stayin' here, I'm gonna do whatever needs done to keep them safe."

Seeing nothing suspicious out front, he walked into the kitchen, grabbed a flashlight from the junk drawer, and went out through the back door to investigate.

He switched the flashlight on and held it flush with his gun as he scanned the trees. Dad slammed the door behind him, clearly disgruntled that he'd been dragged out of bed in the middle of the night, and Marx shot him an irritated look.

"Are you tryin' to wake Mama?"

"If she didn't hear your girl screechin', she ain't gonna hear me shuttin' a door. She's half deaf already, and she sleeps with those plugs in her ears. Says I snore too loud." He jammed a few shells into his shotgun and grumbled, "I don't snore. And this is a waste of time."

"Nobody said you had to come with me. But if you're comin', lock the door." When he didn't move, Marx bounced the flashlight beam toward him. "If you wanna stand guard by the door, fine, but if not . . ."

Dad's jaw shifted, but he opened the door, reached inside to lock it, then pulled it shut again. "Happy?"

"Ecstatic," Marx replied dryly. He moved to the kitchen window, looking for signs of tampering. The lock looked secure, but there was an oily smudge on the glass where someone had pressed their face. "Somebody was here."

"Anythin' could've made that mark. I think your girl's imaginin' things."

"This comin' from the man who's *imaginin'* a love affair between me and a girl young enough to be my daughter?"

Dad made that phlegmy sound of disbelief in the back of his throat. "I know what I see. I've met her kind before."

Marx shined the flashlight directly into his dad's eyes, making him squint. "Her kind? Really?" He shook his head in disgust and started around the house, more to put space between him and his dad than to track down the trespasser.

He doubted his dad had ever met anyone quite like Holly. She had been shuffled through twelve foster homes and spent most of her adult life on the run, trying to stay ahead of her foster brother, who thought she was fun to torment.

Dad's voice followed him around the house. "So you're tellin' me there is nothin' between you two."

Marx's breath left his mouth in a puff of steam, and he turned to confront his dad. "Actually, Dad, there is somethin' between us. I love her. And I don't mean *your* idea of love—the kind that involves beatin' your child and sleepin' around with other women while you're married."

A muscle flexed in Dad's jaw.

Marx may have been a child at the time, but he'd seen Mama cry tears of heartache as she asked God why she wasn't enough for her husband.

"That girl in there,"—Marx pointed toward the house—"the one you arbitrarily decided is no good, is one of the most pure-hearted people I've ever met. Yes, she's beautiful. I'm not blind. But she's more than the way she looks. She's selfless, she's funny, she's adorable, and she's stubborn to a frustratin' fault. Half the time she's more hardheaded than I am. She is everythin' I ever wanted in a daughter, and I couldn't possibly love her more."

Dad gaped at him, dumbfounded. "A daughter? What kind of nonsense are you talkin'—" Something crunched nearby, and Dad's voice cut off, his grip shifting on his gun. "You hear that?"

"Yes, Dad, I'm not deaf."

They visually scanned the yard for the source of the sound, but nothing else moved.

"Can you tell which way it came from?" Dad asked. For somebody who believed the face in the window was nothing but Holly's reflection, he was awfully anxious.

A barely noticeable whisper of a stick or branch snapped behind Marx, and they tracked it back to the trees. The moment Marx illuminated the area with the flashlight, a shape darted from behind the trees and took off across the lawn at a frantic pace.

A boom ricocheted through the night and he cringed, pain splintering through his ears. Dad's wild shot hit a tree and blew off a chunk of bark.

Marx whirled and slapped the barrel of the gun toward the ground. "What is the matter with you?!"

"I'm tired of these thugs traipsin' all over my property like it's an amusement park!"

"It was a rabbit!" Marx ripped the gun from his hands. "You can't just shoot wildly. What if that *had* been a kid? You might've killed him."

"I know where I was aimin'."

"Like you know *not* to fire a gun next to somebody's head?" His ears were still ringing, and he had the beginning of a migraine.

The vein in Dad's forehead throbbed and his fingers curled into fists.

Marx took in the posture that would've sent him running for the cupboard when he was a boy and stepped closer. "What are you gonna do, Dad? Hit me? I'm not a child that you can beat into submission anymore. And this is not a fight you wanna start."

His father vibrated with pent up anger. "I want you out of my house."

"Fine." Marx shoved the shotgun back at him and headed for the front porch.

He was halfway up the steps when his dad let out a curse. He flicked the flashlight toward him, the beam reflecting off the broken beer bottle the kid had chucked into the grass. Dad had stepped on it . . . in slippers.

"Oh for the love of all things holy," Marx muttered. The idea of leaving him to limp back to the house on his own was tempting. Too tempting to be the right thing to do.

He sighed, descended the steps, and crossed the lawn to help his dad, who sputtered a protest the moment Marx ducked under his arm to help lessen the weight on his foot.

"You wanna drive the glass further into your foot, fine. But you can do it in the house." Marx helped the grumbling old fool onto the porch, then called out, "It's safe to open the door."

The door cracked open and Holly peered out, her eyes scanning the darkness behind him for danger. She started to ask a question, but his dad thrust the door the rest of the way open and hobbled past her into the house.

Holly's wary gaze lingered on his back until he disappeared into the living room, then she stepped out onto the porch and folded her arms around herself for warmth. "What happened?"

"We didn't see anybody." When her shoulders dropped in apology, he said, "That doesn't mean somebody wasn't there. They probably just got scared and ran."

"I heard a gunshot."

"My father's a little trigger happy." She looked so worn out, and he wished he could tell her to back upstairs to bed, but unfortunately, that wouldn't be possible. "I know you're tired, sweetheart, but I need you to go get dressed and pack up your things."

7

Now

Maybe I did imagine it.

Holly zipped her suitcase shut harder than necessary at the frustrating possibility.

Sure, occasionally she thought someone was following her and once or twice she may have threatened to mace some leaves, but she wasn't crazy. Sometimes there really *were* footsteps following her or figures lurking outside.

She shuddered at the memory of the masked man crouched in the flowerbed outside her window.

Parting the guestroom curtains, she gazed out into the night. Christmas lights twinkled on rooftops and trees, igniting the nearby street. There was something magical about tiny lights glowing in an ocean of blackness.

Steam from her breath stretched across the glass, and she dragged a fingertip through the moisture, drawing a Christmas tree that faded away as quickly as it appeared.

Christmas was less than a week away. It was more than decorations and store-bought presents, more than sweet treats and hot chocolate. It was a day to honor the most precious gift ever given, a day to be celebrated with family. And after so many years of spending the holidays alone, Holly had been looking forward to at least one family Christmas.

A quiet exhale that bordered on a sigh escaped her as she sank onto the edge of the bed.

She toyed with the faded bracelet engraved with her name that never left her wrist. Thinking about the day she received it always made her smile. She'd been almost nine when she met her best friend in the woods behind her house to exchange Christmas gifts. Jordan had saved his money to have the bracelet made for her, and it had been with her every day since then.

He had decided to stay in New York for Christmas rather than traveling back to Kansas to see his family. It would be such a lonely Christmas. Maybe she would call him when she got to the hotel.

The thought of the hotel brought a heavy sadness with it. It pained her to imagine Marx being so close to home and yet so far from his family on Christmas. She longed for him to reconnect with his parents while there was still time, to build memories that he could cherish long after they passed on.

She couldn't let him throw this opportunity away, especially not because of her. It was obvious that her presence was a point of contention. Mr. Gus didn't want her here. Maybe if she removed herself from the picture, it would help to relieve some of the tension driving Marx and his father apart.

"Is there such a thing as a Christmas wish?" she asked, speaking into the quiet emptiness of the room.

If she could have one wish, it would be healing for Marx and his family. And maybe, just as a little bonus, she would get to decorate a tree with real decorations.

The last tree she decorated had been . . . unique. When you're in a psychiatric facility, they don't let you have hooks or breakable ornaments, wire trees, or . . . well . . . anything that could be used as an implement of harm. But there had been a lot of Elmer's glue, food coloring, and cotton balls.

She pushed off the bed and straightened the blanket, tucking it beneath the edges of the mattress the way it had been when she arrived. She placed Marx's Teddy Bear in between the two pillows. It was such a pathetic-looking little thing, but she could imagine tiny Marx dragging it behind him through the grass or cuddling with it as he fell asleep.

She brushed her thumb over the letters on the bear's foot, still pondering the middle initial. Richard Dewey Marx? She laughed softly to herself. No, that couldn't be it.

Her gaze swept over the room one last time to make sure she had everything before she closed the door.

8

Now

Holly's suitcase thumped down every step as she half-carried, half-dragged it down the stairs. When she finally reached the foyer, she puffed out a tired breath and dropped the suitcase to the floor.

She tucked her hands into the pouch of her oversized sweatshirt and shuffled across the hall into the living room in her purple rain boots and thick gray leggings. It looked like someone had lopped off the arms of a cable knit sweater and pulled them up over her legs.

"Pick up your feet when you walk," Dad snapped, glaring at her as she entered the room.

She took a few exaggerated, stomping steps and then lifted her eyebrows at him as if to say, "is that what you had in mind?"

Dad lowered his head and grumbled into his chest about disobedient brats, but Holly chose to ignore it. She tilted her head at Marx, who was kneeling on the floor in front of his dad's chair. "What happened?"

"He stepped on a piece of glass outside." Marx popped open the first-aid kit he'd retrieved from the bathroom.

"The beer bottle?"

Dad latched onto her words like they were an admission of guilt. "You threw that bottle in my yard so I would step on it?"

"Do you even hear yourself?" Marx asked, astounded by his father's ability to make wild assumptions based on nothing.

"It was a perfectly legitimate question."

"Maybe, if you were accusin' me instead of Holly."

He pulled the tweezers from the first-aid kit. There was a shard of glass protruding from the bottom of Dad's slipper, and he was going to have to remove it before he could do anything else.

Headlights glinted off the living room window and Marx stretched up on his knees to see a cab driver pulling into the driveway. "Why is there a taxi in the driveway?" He looked over at Holly, who shifted her feet and dropped her gaze to the floor. "Holly, what's goin' on?"

She cleared her throat. "I'm gonna stay in a hotel."

"*We* are stayin' in a hotel," he corrected. "Just as soon as I'm done here."

She shook her head. "I don't want you to come with me. I want you to stay here with your family. I think . . . maybe things will go better if . . ." she glanced at his dad. "If I'm not here."

Dad grunted. "So she does have a brain."

Tired of his rudeness, Marx grabbed the piece of glass with the tweezers and ripped it out of Dad's foot without warning. Dad let out a string of profanity that would make a nun faint.

"Augustus Gray!" The voice snapped through the upstairs hallway like a whip, and Dad jerked, his head twisting toward the staircase.

Marx wasn't the least bit surprised by Mama's sudden appearance or the air of authority her voice carried. Even in a fluffy robe with curlers in her hair, she could make a grown man tremble in his boots.

She stomped down the steps, her lips puckered in outraged disappointment, and shook a finger at his dad. "I don't ever wanna hear that kind of language come from your mouth again."

Dad straightened on the couch, preparing for a fight. "I had glass in my foot! Besides, this is my house, and I'll speak however I please."

Holly offered Marx a wide-eyed *did-he-just-say-that* look. After all these years, Dad should've known better, but clearly he was as dense as a tree stump.

Mama mounted her hands on her hips. "Your house? Is that so?"

Her tone warned of dangerous waters ahead, but Dad tripped and fell right off the pier. "You heard what I said."

Marx stood and took Holly by the arm, leading her into the kitchen for privacy.

She pulled free from his grip the moment they stepped onto the tile. "I have to do this."

"No, you don't. Either we both stay or we both go. I'm not lettin' you stay in a hotel by yourself."

She drew herself up defiantly, trying to appear taller. "I'm not a child. I can take care of myself."

"Are you standin' on your tiptoes?" He looked down at her feet. "You are."

She deflated with a huff, dropping her feet flat on the floor. She wanted so badly to be bigger than she was, but she wouldn't be getting taller anytime soon.

"Look, sweetheart, this isn't about you bein' incapable of takin' care of yourself. I know you're capable." He'd been working with her in his spare time to make *sure* she was capable.

"Then let me stay in a hotel."

"Holly, if I wanted to spend a week alone with my parents, I would've left you in New York. I brought you here so that we could all have Christmas together. As a family."

"Then why do you wanna leave?"

"Because my dad has made it perfectly clear that he doesn't want me here."

"But your mom does. And I do. Isn't that enough?" She looked up at him with those heart-melting brown eyes, waiting for him to tell her no, that she wasn't reason enough to stay.

His resolve crumbled, and he wrapped his arms around her, pulling her into a tight hug. "You're always enough, sweet pea." He didn't want her to ever doubt that. "And if it means that much to you, then we'll stay. No matter what my dad says."

She mumbled something into his chest that might have been "okay," but it was too muffled to tell.

"Let's go get your suitcase back upstairs before Mama sees it and has a conniption fit."

She drew back with a befuddled expression. "A what?"

"A hysterical episode."

"Oh. You should just say that next time."

He chuckled as they walked back down the hall. She was always complaining about the words he used, usually because she didn't know what they meant.

His parents were still bickering, and Dad was struggling to gain the upper hand. "I'm the head of this household. And I say what goes."

"Just 'cause your head's bigger don't make you the head of the household," Mama shot back. "But if you insist on bein' the head, and it's 'your house,' then I guess you better start cleanin' it. While you're at it, cook your own dinner. And don't forget the dishes. They ain't gonna wash themselves."

"You're talkin' nonsense, woman."

"And when you do the laundry," she continued. "Don't mix the whites with the colors. You'll end up with pink underwear. 'Course that might suit you just fine since you've takin' to throwin' tantrums like a two year old girl."

"I am not throwin' tantrums!" Dad shouted.

Mama lifted incredulous eyebrows. "You most certainly are. Ever since they arrived, you been slammin' things, shoutin' your protests to kingdom come, and don't think I didn't hear that gunshot. It certainly wasn't thunder."

"Now listen here, woman—"

Mama lifted a warning finger. "*Woman* me one more time, Augustus, and I'm gonna send you to the dentist."

Holly leaned closer to Marx and whispered, "She's awesome."

His mama was certainly a force to be reckoned with, and Dad was ill-equipped. He looked down at Holly and asked, "Are you takin' notes?"

"Yep." She raised a fist in the air and whispered in her best Southern accent, "*Peanut* me one more time."

Marx choked back a laugh. With her feisty spirit, she would fit right in with his Southern family.

A horn honked outside.

Realizing that the cabbie was still waiting for his fare, Marx excused himself and stepped outside to send the driver on his way.

The sun crept over the horizon as Marx sat on the porch steps, rubbing a blade of grass between his fingers.

It was strange being back. It was like nothing had changed—he slept in the same bed, watched the sun rise over the same trees, and ghosted down the same halls to avoid his dad.

But in truth, nothing was exactly the way he remembered.

The years had changed all of them. Mama's meekness had worn away to reveal a hidden strength beneath and Dad, who was living on borrowed time with his failing heart, had finally cast aside his drinking.

And *he* had changed, too. The tender-hearted and soft-spoken boy he had once been was gone. The injustices of the world had hardened him and sharpened his soft-spoken voice into one that demanded to be heard and obeyed.

That was the man he was when he met Holly, and he would never forget the way he shouted at her and slammed things when she wouldn't give him the information he wanted. It was in that moment, as she cowered from him with terror and tears in her eyes, that he realized just how much like his father he'd become.

The revelation had shaken him, and he spent the rest of that night retracing the steps of his life to figure out where and when he had stumbled into his dad's shoes. He never intended to become that man, to demand compliance through fear.

The next day, he forced himself to do something his dad never would; he humbled himself before the person he'd hurt and asked for forgiveness.

Holly, who trusted men about as far as she could push them, forgave him and welcomed him back into her life. He wished he was capable of extending that kind of grace to another person.

How do I make this work, Lord? It's five days until Christmas. A hundred and twenty hours in a house with a man who wants nothin' more than to kick me out the door.

He flicked the blade of grass away, watching it disappear into the overgrown yard, and waited for an answer to descend from on high. But his silent question was met with an equally silent answer.

As much as he didn't want to dance around his dad to keep the peace, he didn't see another choice.

At least now, he was big enough to stand up to the man who made his childhood miserable. Some people—people like Holly—would never have that advantage. She would always be smaller than the man who hurt her.

He pushed to his feet and crossed the yard to find the bottle Dad had stepped on early this morning before Mama or Holly happened across it with the same unfortunate consequence.

As he gathered the largest pieces of glass in his hand, he noticed the old garage out back. If his parents still kept the key on the kitchen wall by the fridge, he could unlock the garage and get to the mower. It had been a long time since anyone tended to this grass.

He tossed the pieces of bottle into the garbage and went to grab the key. He paused when he found two sets dangling from the hook, and he stared at the second ring as he tried to recall what the key belonged to.

He found out once he unlocked the garage door and pushed it open. A 1951 Chevy sat in the middle of the room beneath a tarp.

Dad's old truck.

Marx had fallen in love with that truck when he was a boy and had even asked if he could fix it up—a mistake he didn't make twice. He never understood why Dad would leave such a work of art to collect dust.

A man's car could give him a sense of pride and status, and a lot of time and work went into maintaining them. It wasn't unusual to cover them to protect them from the elements, but for as far back as he could remember, this truck had been beneath some kind of cover. He suspected it was less to protect the paint and more because Dad couldn't bear the sight of it.

He peeled back the tarp and ran a hand over the beautiful curves of the classic's hood.

He'd snuck into it once when he was a teenager, but Dad caught him and dragged him back out, whipping him so badly that it hurt to move for a week.

Marx took pride in his car, but at the end of the day, it was just a hunk of metal on wheels. It wasn't worth hurting somebody over.

Holly was a catastrophe behind the wheel of his car. She could hit a tree twenty feet from the road. It wasn't that she was incapable of staying between the lines, but she was distracted by every little thing. Teaching her to drive left more dings and scratches on his car than ever before, but he never snapped the way his dad did.

The simple fact was that he valued Holly far more than his car.

He smiled, remembering the day she took out a handicap sign because a bird flew into the windshield. She bit her bottom lip and shrank down in the driver's seat, as if no one would notice, and he'd laughed.

Thankfully she hadn't caused any serious damage to the car or them. The same couldn't be said for the handicap sign.

He ran a hand over the windshield of the old truck. He'd always wondered what caused the crack in the windshield and the large dents in the front bumper and truck bed, but he knew better than to ask.

He opened the driver's door and slid in to the old cab. It was simpler inside than it was on the outside, but it was still a work of art. He was tempted to slip the key into the ignition and turn over the engine, but he knew that wouldn't be a good idea.

Something about this truck haunted his dad. It was more than just pride or the desire to preserve a classic that drove him to lock it away in a garage beneath a tarp, to forbid anyone to touch it or ask about it. It was almost as though he feared it.

8

Then

Gus groaned as he lifted his head off the steering wheel, pain splitting through his skull. For a moment, he sat dazed, blinking through the cracked windshield at the rain pattering across the hood of the truck.

His eyes traced the zigzagging crack that spanned the windshield. How had that happened?

Did I hit something?

Just as the thought skittered through his brain, the accident came rushing back: the little girl in the road, the wheels gliding across the water-drenched street, the jolt as the truck hit something.

"God, no. Please no."

His hands shook as he opened the driver's door and climbed out into the rain. What if she was dead? What if he'd killed her? His foot slipped, and he landed hard on the road, every joint in his body screaming in agony.

He spat muddy rain water from his mouth and blinked to clear his vision. A ragdoll lay in the puddle just inches from his face, and horror collided with the panic in his chest when he recognized it.

It couldn't be. It wasn't possible. Martha would never have let her go outside alone, especially not in the rain. He grabbed a hold of the doll and dragged it closer. Hand stitched into the doll's foot were the initials CAM.

His stomach tried to push itself up his throat and out onto the pavement, but he fought it back and stumbled to his feet. He had to find her.

"Cressy!"

His baby girl was only three, and the truck . . .

He stopped when saw a flash of white in the ditch, torn between the desperation to go to her and terror of what he would find. He staggered forward on stiff legs.

A ragged sob escaped his throat and he collapsed to his knees by the ditch. "Cressy." He gathered her limp body into his arms.

He'd known the moment he saw the doll, but now that he held her and gazed into her sweet face, every trace of hope shattered. Grief tore through him and he screamed into the night with rage and pain as he rocked the body of his baby girl.

10

Now

The chains creaked as Gus rocked on the porch swing. He gripped a mug of coffee between both hands, letting the heat soothe the arthritic ache in his swollen knuckles.

He hated getting old almost as much as he hated the coffee in his mug—foul decaf sludge—but Martha wouldn't allow him to have regular coffee. The caffeine, along with anything else that tasted good, was off the menu with his heart condition.

He tried to sneak out of the house with a regular coffee this morning, but the woman was like a bloodhound; she could sniff out his sneakiness from across the house, and she snatched the mug from his fingers before he made it outside.

Why she was so dead set on keeping him alive, he would never know. Not like anyone would really miss him if he kicked the bucket.

He took another sip of coffee, wishing it were something strong enough to take the edge off the memories clawing their way back from the grave. He could feel the icy chill of them raking down his spine as he thought about the face Holly claimed to have seen in the window.

That was how it began before. The eyes peering through an opening in the drapes, the footsteps on the porch, the pounding on the door in the middle of the night.

He'd seen the fear in Martha's eyes when he told her about the man outside the kitchen window.

He couldn't let that happen to his family, not again. He just hoped that the mysterious face in the window had been a figment of Holly's imagination.

His attention drifted toward her as she gathered eggs from the yard and placed them gently into the basket Martha had given her.

She was an odd girl, her manner shifting as easily as the breeze. One moment she was humming while picking up eggs, and the next she was looking over her shoulder for something that wasn't there.

His son's words from last night rang through his mind: *she is everythin' I ever wanted in a daughter.*

Despite the twenty year age gap between Richard and Holly, Gus just couldn't wrap his mind around the notion that there was nothing romantic between them. She wasn't blood, she wasn't a child, and she was far from homely. This paternal relationship Richard claimed to have with her didn't make sense. It wasn't natural.

Or maybe you're just makin' it too personal.

The face of a beautiful young woman materialized in his mind—brown eyes and midnight hair with a sensuality that lured him into her bed. He couldn't even remember her name, or maybe she had never given it. But she had to be eighteen or twenty years younger than him when they spent the night together. It hadn't mattered to either of them: the age difference or the intimacy.

He left her hotel room feeling emptier than he had when he entered it, as though those intimate moments with a stranger had stolen something precious.

Martha forgave him because she understood his brokenness, but those moments he spent seeking comfort from other women ate away at the trust between husband and wife, and slowly began to dissolve his relationship with God. He was supposed to lead his family in God's ways, but he was dishonoring his wife.

It took him a long while to get his life on track, but Martha walked alongside him every stumbling step of the way. She was the greatest gift God had ever given him, and he regretted all the years he didn't appreciate her.

"Hey, old timer."

Gus groaned inwardly as Alex Martin, their neighbor, strolled across the lawn in holey jeans and some rock band T-shirt that looked like it hadn't been washed in days. "What do you want?"

Alex grinned, showing teeth caked with every meal he'd had for the past month. "I heard there was some trouble last night while I was out."

He clomped up the steps in his muddy boots and flopped onto the empty side of the swing without invitation. He reeked, and it made Gus's nose hairs curl.

"Get off my swing."

Alex sprawled leisurely. "Now is that any way to treat the kindhearted neighbor who brought you a beer?" He dangled the bottle between them.

Gus's mouth instinctively watered as he stared at the offering. Alcohol had been the balm for his wounds for over half his life, and with the memories of that painful night clawing their way back to the surface, it took all his willpower not to reach out and take it.

He swallowed and forced words from his throat. "I quit drinkin'."

"It's just one beer. What the old lady don't know . . ."

He watched the liquid slosh in the bottle as he considered Alex's words. He could probably get away with one beer, but it wasn't worth breaking his promise to Martha, and it definitely wasn't worth seeing the disappointment in her eyes.

"Take your temptation and get off my porch."

Alex laughed. He had been their neighbor long enough to know that Gus struggled with alcoholism, and this was fun for him. "Boy, your old lady got you tamed."

"I want you off my property."

"And I want you to hurry up and die of a heart attack, but I guess we're both gonna be disappointed."

Alex took a swig of his beer and wiped a hand across his chin to catch the bit that dribbled down.

"Your grandparents were nice people. Your parents, too. Somethin' went wrong with you."

Alex was a thirty two year old man who spent his days hanging around with teenagers, drinking until he couldn't walk straight and partying until dawn.

Alex leaned forward on the swing. "Ain't nothin' wrong with me. I'm just livin' my life."

"You're *wastin'* your life. Take advice from somebody who's been where you are."

"I don't want or need your advice, Gramps. And I don't want you sendin' your boy over, breakin' up my parties like he did last night."

Gus had no idea what he was talking about. He hadn't sent Richard anywhere. But he lifted his chin and stared the kid down. "You're lucky it was just my son. Next time we'll call the cops."

Not that the cops had done anything thus far. He knew Alex and those kids were responsible for the incidents on their property: the smashed mailbox, decorations being torn down, the house being egged. He just couldn't prove it, and neither could the detective who took their statements.

"I'd be careful, if I were you, old timer. All kinds of bad things can happen to people who don't mind their own business in this neighborhood. Wouldn't want you or the Misses fallin' and breakin' a bone. I hear that's how old folks end up in nursin' homes, medicated 'til they die."

Gus's temper boiled. Nobody threatened his wife. "You come near my family and I'll—"

"Don't go gettin' all worked up. We was just havin' a nice conversation." Alex took another long pull of his beer. "That's a nice new lawn ornament you got there."

Gus followed his gaze to Holly. She must have sensed that she was being watched, because she looked their way.

"I think I might introduce myself." Alex rose from the swing and left the beer behind as he stepped off the porch and started across the grass, a swagger in his step.

Gus debated whether or not to intervene, but Holly was a grown woman; surely, she could handle the situation.

Alex closed in, his gaze slithering over her from head to toe. "Ain't you the finest thing I ever seen."

Gus almost snorted coffee through his nose. That was a line, if ever he'd heard one. Of course, the first thing he said to Martha when they met hadn't been much better. He told her that he hoped she knew First-Aid, because she was so beautiful he might pass out. She laughed and then asked him to dinner.

He watched Holly to see how she would react. He had yet to see her sway her hips or flaunt her curves, and there wasn't a trace of sensuality in the way she carried herself. If anything, she looked . . . awkward and uncomfortable in her skin. Like a fat kid whose clothes were too tight, which made no sense, because she was skinny as a toothpick.

Her shoulders stiffened, and she regarded Alex warily, clearly unmoved by his attempt to be charming.

"I ain't never seen eyes so pretty." Alex reached a hand toward her face, as if to touch her, and she flinched away. "Bet you get compliments all the time."

Gus sat forward on the swing. Something didn't feel right about the way this interaction was unfolding. The girl didn't seem disinterested or annoyed with the advances; she seemed . . . uneasy.

"I have to go." Holly gave Alex a wide berth as she made a beeline for the porch.

Alex followed, his long legs devouring the space she hastened to put between them. "Hey." He cut her off before she could reach the steps, and she sucked in an audible breath. "I paid you a compliment. Least you could do is gimme a little conversation."

She tried to go around him, but he stepped closer, backing her up against the side of the house. "Please," she said, visibly starting to tremble. "I j-just . . . wanna be left alone."

Gus stood and gripped the porch railing. He might not be fond of the girl, but she was clearly frightened, and he wasn't the kind of man to sit by and watch a girl be harassed. "That's enough. Give the girl her space."

Alex sneered at him. "Or what, old man? You gonna grab your cane and beat me over the head with it?"

The insult singed Gus's pride. He knew he was old, and he wouldn't fare too good in a scuffle with someone half his age. Unless he went inside to grab his gun. He caught Holly's wandering gaze, and the desperation and fear in her eyes forced him to make a decision.

He hollered for Richard and hoped that he would show up before things got out of hand.

"You don't gotta stay in this retirement home," Alex said. "I got room. And my place is a lot more fun." He rested his hands suggestively on her narrow hips, and Holly went off like a firecracker.

She kicked him and started bashing the basket of eggs against his head.

Richard sprinted around the side of the house, took one look at the situation, and launched into action. He grabbed Holly around the middle and hauled her away from the man she was trying to beat to death with broken eggs.

Alex let out a string of foul names as he swiped a hand through the dozen eggs oozing down his face.

Richard struggled to keep a hold of Holly, who was as a slippery as a fish, and threw a warning glare Alex's way. "Keep runnin' your mouth and *I'm* gonna hit you next. And I hit a lot harder than she does."

Alex backed away and then fled back to his own property, tripping and falling up his back steps in his rush to get inside.

Richard sank to his knees in the grass, wrapping Holly in a hold that was more comforting than restricting. "Sh, you're all right, sweetheart."

She curled into him as she struggled to breathe between heavy sobs, and Richard rested his chin on top of her head.

Gus's eyes trailed to an object in the grass a few feet from where they knelt, and a fiery anger rolled through him. He stomped down the steps and snatched up the key to his truck, then walked back inside and shut the door.

11

Now

Gus tossed the keys into the junk drawer in the kitchen and slammed the drawer, anger and anxiety coursing through him.

Richard had always tested his boundaries as a boy, but he had never been blatantly disrespectful. Not like this. He knew Gus didn't want him anywhere near that truck, and he defied his wishes anyway.

He swatted the box of toothpicks across the counter, so angry he could barely think straight.

Martha wanted him to tell Richard the truth, but in the wrong hands, the truth could destroy their lives. How could he entrust it to somebody who didn't even respect him?

Unless he already knew . . .

What had Holly said last night? *I know what you did. And maybe you should think twice before throwing around words like coward.*

The only way Holly could know anything about his family was because Richard told her. Maybe his son *did* know. Maybe he'd overheard something when he was a boy, and that was why he left.

Gus straightened when heavy footsteps came down the hall toward the kitchen. Richard walked past him to the sink, flipping on the faucet to wash off the egg slime coating his forearms.

His gaze glossed over the scattered toothpicks, and he let out a soft grunt of amusement. "I see the toothpicks looked at you wrong. At least I assume that's why you knocked 'em across the room."

Gus grimaced. "I told you never to mess with my truck."

Richard dried his hands and grabbed a coffee mug from the cupboard. "You told me a lot of things." He filled it with water and placed it in the microwave. "What is it with you and that truck anyway?"

"That's my business."

"Fine." He fingered through Martha's tea tin until he found the flavor he was searching for, then leaned against the counter, waiting for the water to warm.

Silence stretched through the kitchen, disturbed only by the constant drip of the faucet and the quiet hum of the microwave.

The timer ticked steadily downward, the seconds seeming to drag by as the silence lengthened.

When Martha first told Gus that he was going to be a father, he never imagined this day. Less than two feet from his own child without a word to say to one another.

He cleared his throat and nodded to the peppermint tea bag dangling from Richard's fingers. "Nauseous?"

"Holly's got an upset stomach."

Judging by the way the girl nearly hyperventilated in the front yard, Gus suspected it was nerves irritating the lining of her stomach. "She all right?"

Richard slid him a sideways glance, as if trying to decide whether or not he really cared. "She will be."

"I ain't never seen nobody react the way she did when Alex put his hands on her."

"She has her reasons."

Gus paused to consider how he wanted to phrase his question. "Somethin' bad happen to her?"

A shadow of pain darkened Richard's eyes, and he fixed his attention on the tea bag in his hand. "You could say that."

Gus recognized the sense of guilt interwoven with his son's pain because it was something he'd wrestled with every day since that long-ago night. "Was it . . . somethin' you did?"

"Why do you care all the sudden? You don't even like her, and you've never been interested in my life."

"I'm just makin' polite conversation."

"Well don't."

"Fine. I won't."

He could ask Martha for the details about the girl, though he wasn't sure she'd tell him. Every time she brought Holly up, Gus had ended the conversation. He hadn't wanted to hear about the girl he believed was his son's mistress.

The microwave beeped and Richard retrieved the mug, adding a squirt of honey before dropping the tea bag into the steaming water.

"What's wrong with her?" Gus asked, the question snagging Richard's attention before he could leave the room.

He stopped just short of the hallway and turned back. "*Nothin'* is wrong with her. And don't you dare suggest somethin' is."

Gus wrestled back the anger that surged up at the disrespect in his son's tone. "Well she ain't right. Normal folks don't act the way she does."

"Just because she's not fond of men doesn't mean there's somethin' wrong with her. She's been hurt. A lot."

"She seems to trust you just fine."

"I worked very hard to earn that trust. Now if we're done pretendin' to be civil, I have somewhere else I'd rather be." He walked out.

Gus dragged his hands over his face in exasperation and shook his head. "Why, Lord? Why did You give me a son who's—"

"A spittin' image?" Martha stepped out of the basement stairwell with two jars of homemade soup.

"Maybe He thought you'd understand each other better. Unfortunately, that backfired."

"We are nothin' alike."

Martha gathered the scattered toothpicks into a pile. "He certainly didn't learn to be angry and distant from me."

Gus crossed his arms. "I am not angry and distant."

"Mmm hmm. Bitter as unsweet tea, too." She pulled the ingredients out of the cupboard for cornbread, listing them off under her breath to make sure she didn't miss any.

Gus fished her cornbread pan out of the cupboard above the fridge and set it on the counter with a scowl. "I ain't bitter."

"Just sour on occasion?"

He gave that one some thought. "Only in the mornin's when you snitch my coffee and give me that decaf poison."

She smiled and kissed his cheek. "And I'm gonna do it every mornin', 'cause I intend on keepin' you around a while longer."

"A while?"

"Maybe 'til Christmas, if you behave yourself."

"You still ain't told me what you want for Christmas."

She set a brick of butter on the counter, her lighthearted mood turning serious. "You know what I want for Christmas, Gus. It's been far too long, and we don't got that many years left."

"What am I supposed to do?"

"*Talk* to him. Make things right. I want my family whole. That's all I've ever wanted."

"I tried talkin' to him, Martha. He don't listen."

"Then try harder."

"He's the one who walked away, not me."

Martha sighed and rested her hands on the counter. She didn't say anything for a long moment, but the quiet sniff told him she was fighting back the urge to cry. "Maybe you're right. Maybe it's just too late."

Martha was the hopeful one, always willing to believe there was a way. He didn't want to be the reason she lost that hope. "Martha . . ."

She waved him off and went to work on the cornbread, throwing herself into a distraction to avoid the hurt he'd caused. He started to give her the space she wanted, but she spoke before he made it out of the kitchen.

"You know, Gus, whether you realize it or not, you hurt our boy." She looked at him, her green eyes shimmering with unshed tears. "You stand there and tell me that he don't listen and that he walks away. But you're the one who hardened his heart."

"What are you sayin'?"

She drew in a breath and let it out before continuing. "You were not the father he deserved, Gus."

Her words pounded into him like a physical blow, each one impacting his chest. Not the father he deserved?

"I know this is hard for you to understand. I know you believe you did everythin' right. But if you're gonna fix this, if you're gonna make things right, you need to show him the tenderness and love that he needed from you when he was a boy. Be the father he needs you to be."

12

Then

Fresh tears mingled with the rain on Gus's face as he trudged up the dirt and gravel drive toward the house. A patch of mud at the bottom had sucked his left shoe right off his foot, but he didn't have the time or the energy to stop and put it back on. He needed to get to the house and call an ambulance, even though he feared it was too late.

He cradled Cressy's body against his chest as he pushed on toward the top of the hill, his guilt and despair heavier than the sopping wet clothes he wore.

"Why, Lord?"

He looked down at his baby's face—the curve of her little button nose, the dark eyebrows that bunched together when she didn't get her way, the pink lips that could melt his resolve with a smile. Her face was perfectly still, as though she were already gone.

"Why didn't you just take me? Why my baby?"

The shuddering breath he drew in as he reached the yard caught in his lungs. A brown truck was parked in the grass by the shed, and the front door to the house stood wide open. He knew that truck. But why was it here? Where was Martha?

His sluggish brain was still trying to make sense of what he was seeing when a woman screamed somewhere in the house.

13

Now

Holly sat in the living room chair, her feet drawn up onto the cushion and her arms wrapped around her stomach.

Marx handed her the mug of hot peppermint tea and crouched in front of her, resting his hands on her rainbow-socked feet. "You did nothin' wrong, sweetheart."

He hadn't witnessed the events leading up to the panic attack and she hadn't shared them, but Holly wasn't a violent person. The man must've done something to make her feel threatened.

The only reason Marx wasn't kicking his door down was because Holly insisted she wasn't hurt, and he had no evidence to the contrary.

She let out a quiet breath and stared into the mug of tea. Although she said nothing, he could read the frustration on her face.

Her panic attacks were becoming less frequent as God and time knitted her spirit back together, and it had been nearly a month since her last one.

"I know it feels like you've taken a step back, but one panic attack does not send you back to where you started, sweet pea."

She looked at him, her eyes red-rimmed from the pressure of tears she was determined not to shed.

"You've come a long way, and you're stronger for it. That doesn't mean there won't be the occasional bump in the road, but you know that when you hit it, God and I are gonna be there."

An unmarked car pulled into the driveway and a black man with graying hair stepped out.

Now what?

The man took in the property with a sweep of his eyes before closing his car door.

Marx stood. "I'm gonna go see who's here." He fetched a blanket from the rack near the fireplace and wrapped it around Holly, covering her from chin to toes. "Drink your tea. It'll calm your stomach." He kissed the top of her head before leaving to check on the visitor.

The smell of cigarette smoke wafted through the screen door into the house, but when Marx stepped out onto the porch, the man was no longer in the driveway.

He descended the steps and approached the unfamiliar black sedan. There was no one else inside the car, but there was a cigarette smoldering in the ashtray.

Was the guy just wandering around the property? In light of what happened last night, that was a dangerous thing to do.

Marx hoped he wouldn't have to shoot anybody this afternoon. That would put a damper on the Christmas holiday.

The scent of cigarette smoke led him around to the back of the house, where the stranger crouched beneath the kitchen window, poking around in Mama's flowerbed.

Marx gripped the butt of his gun, prepared to draw it at a moment's notice. "There better be a good reason you're on my family's property."

The man looked up, his gaze immediately snapping to the gun on Marx's hip, and reached for his own weapon as he shot to his feet. He barely had a chance to touch his weapon before Marx had his drawn and aimed at his chest.

"Hands."

The man released his weapon and lifted both hands into the air, surprise flickering across his face. "Rick?"

It took Marx a second to connect the lean, middle-aged man to the chubby, baby-faced teenager he'd befriended as a child. "Darian?"

The smile that crossed the man's face melted away the years, revealing the boy Marx had spent most of his youth with. "Can I put my hands down now?"

Marx nodded and lowered his gun to his side, but he didn't holster it. A person could change a lot in thirty years, and there was no guarantee this man was anything like the boy he remembered.

Darian dropped his arms and readjusted the gray suit he wore. "Your mama told me you was a cop, too."

"Too?"

Darian nudged aside his jacket to reveal his badge. "Georgia P.D. Twenty years. Why you think I'm wearin' a suit?"

"I figured somebody died." Darian's mama had barely been able to convince him to wear shoes when they were kids, let alone a suit. Easter Sunday had been torture.

"Close enough. This thing's apt to strangle me to death." He tugged at the tie around his neck. "Like a fancy leash the bosses use to jerk me around."

Marx grunted as he slid his weapon back into the holster. He knew the feeling.

Darian took his measure with a brisk head-to-toe sweep of his eyes. "Man, I hate to say it, but you grew up better lookin' than me."

"Mmm hmm."

"I still got a better tan though."

Marx cracked a smile. When they were boys, he would come home burnt to a crisp after hours of playing outside, but Darian looked no worse for wear. "I'm surprised you became a cop. I seem to remember you bein' on the wrong side of the law more often than not."

Darian bobbed his head in a so-so gesture. "Ain't like you never done nothin' wrong. You remember the time you loosened all the screws on our math teacher's chair? Thing fell apart like a house of cards the moment he tried to squeeze into it."

"I remember. He accused me of cheatin' on a test when I didn't, then called my parents in for a meetin'. I got a beatin' that night." He thought it only fair that it hurt both of them to sit the next day. "I assume you're not wanderin' around my family's property because you've taken up voyeurism as a hobby. So what brings you by?"

"I called him." Mama stepped outside through the back door of the kitchen with a tray of cookies and hot coffee.

She smiled as she handed each of them a mug, but it didn't reach her eyes—eyes that shimmered with the same unease he'd seen in Dad's eyes earlier this morning.

Marx accepted the coffee. "Is this about the face Holly saw outside the window?"

"Your daddy mentioned it, and I know y'all didn't find nothin' when you went out lookin', but it don't hurt to be thorough."

Darian grabbed a couple cookies from the tray before she set it aside. He muttered his gratitude around a mouthful of cookie and brushed the crumbs from his tie. "The ground was too dry last night to capture footprints, but the weeds around the house are crushed."

Marx crouched to examine the area that had held Darian's attention when he first came around the house. He'd noticed the smudge on the window last night, but the trampled weeds hadn't been visible in the darkness. Someone had been creeping along the edge of the house.

"Is there any reason somebody might wanna be lookin' through your family's windows?"

Mama rubbed her arms as though Darian's question chilled her. "Goodness, I don't know."

"There've been a rash of robberies in the area lately. Probably 'cause of the holidays. It's possible—"

Mama broke in. "We ain't got nothin' worth stealin', Darian, and you know it. You been in our home enough to know that our wealth ain't in material things."

"Yes, ma'am. Is there anythin' else that might've attracted somebody to the house?"

Marx caught Mama's gaze as he straightened, and he was certain he saw the same thought pass behind her eyes. Holly was the only person who saw the man outside of the window, possibly because *she* was what he was watching.

He walked around the house to the front yard, his attention fixed on the back door that Alex Martin had scampered into this morning. If the man had the nerve to waltz onto his family's property during the day and harass his family, Marx doubted he had any reservations about doing it at night.

Mama appeared beside him and rested a hand on his arm. "You don't think Alex . . ."

"I *do* think Alex."

Darian puckered his lips in thought as he filled the open space to Marx's left. "It could just be neighborhood kids. With the other nuisance problems you've had—"

"What nuisance problems?" Marx looked from Darian to Mama, pinning her with a demanding look. "Mama."

"It ain't nothin' you need to worry about."

"You really gonna make me ask Dad?"

Her lips pinched into a frown, but she sighed. "He'll just exaggerate everythin'." She waved a hand at Darian, giving him permission to explain.

"I been over a few times to check into some minor issues—the mailbox bein' knocked off and smashed, the house bein' egged, decorations torn down. All things kids tend to do when they're out lookin' to have fun."

"Or when they're drunk." Marx eyed the firepit where he had found the group of kids last night, chugging down beers and listening to that pulsating noise they called music.

"What makes you think the neighbor's involved?"

"Because he was over here causin' problems this mornin'. I don't know exactly what happened, but he did somethin' to upset Holly."

14

Now

Gus grabbed his jacket from the closet under the stairs and pulled it on over his flannel shirt. A brisk walk was sure to clear his mind.

Martha's words ricocheted around in his body like a stray bullet, puncturing his heart, his pride, his nerves, and anything else that got in its way.

You were not the father he deserved.

But he'd been the best father he could be. What more was there? It just didn't make sense. He'd done everything he could possibly do to raise his son proper.

As he closed the closet door, his gaze snagged on the girl curled up in his recliner. She was so fair-skinned that the flames crackling in the fireplace reflected off her face, and the stillness of her expression made him wonder what she was thinking about.

He glanced at the front door, torn between going for his walk and getting to know the girl who inspired so much love and loyalty from his son.

He supposed the polite thing to do would be to check on her.

The old floorboards betrayed his approach, and she followed his movements with wary eyes until he settled on the end of the couch. She didn't trust him, and judging by the way she curled deeper into his chair, she didn't want him coming any closer.

"I ain't gonna hurt you girl."

He had never hurt a woman in his life, but he was beginning to suspect *somebody* had hurt this girl. The incident with Alex had rattled her, and the force of personality he'd seen in her last night as she glared at him from the second floor was gone, making her seem even tinier and more delicate.

He cleared his throat and tried to think of something to say. "How's your stomach?"

"Fine. Just nerves."

He'd figured as much. "Alex scared you pretty good."

"He just . . . caught me off guard." She tugged the blanket tighter around her. "I'm sorry about the eggs."

She had wasted a good dozen eggs over that fool's filthy head, but he couldn't bring himself to scold her for it. She was already as jumpy as a rabbit. "I expect the chickens will lay more."

She blinked. "Was that . . . a joke?"

"Was it funny?"

"Not really."

"Then no, I suppose it wasn't."

Her lips twitched into a small, awkward smile, but it didn't stay long. "I, um . . . I wanted to thank you. For trying to help earlier."

"Nothin' to thank me for. Anybody else would've done the same."

A sad smile touched her lips. "I wish that were true." She gazed back into the fireplace, but her eyes were distant, as if she'd fallen into a memory.

"What makes you say that?"

"About a day after my foster brother abducted me, there was a man who saw me trying to escape. He didn't help. He didn't say a word. Not until three days later when Marx offered a reward for information. If he had just said something, Marx would've found me three sooner."

Gus's throat was so tight that he could hardly swallow. Now the sadness and fear made sense. "When?"

She dabbed at her nose with the sleeve of her sweatshirt. "When you had your last heart attack."

Gus sat straighter. His heart attack had been this past March, which meant she had been taken just nine months ago. "My son was here. He came to the hospital to check on me, but then he got a phone call and he left. In a hurry. That phone call was about you?"

She nodded. "If he hadn't been so determined to find me, if he hadn't used his own money as a reward . . . I don't . . . think I would be here."

He'd been furious with Richard for leaving, assuming that he didn't care enough about his family to stay. But he hadn't realized a girl's life was on the line. *This* girl's life. "He must really love you."

She smiled. "And you."

The front door opened and Richard stepped inside with Detective Darian. They made their way into the living room to get the details about this morning's incident, and Martha followed with a tray of sweets.

15

Then

I won't let him hurt my family.

Broken glass crunched beneath Gus's feet as he crept down the hall toward the closet under the stairs. It broke his heart to leave Cressy's body outside, but he needed both hands to protect the rest of his family.

Martha yelped in the kitchen and fear twisted Gus's intestines into knots. What was he doing to Martha? He knew the man in his kitchen was capable of unspeakable violence, and he couldn't let himself imagine what was happening. He needed to focus his mind and his nerves.

He opened the closet and groped for the string swinging from the ceiling. It brushed against the side of his hand and he yanked it, switching on the bulb.

He grabbed his rifle off the wall and pulled down the box of bullets, his wet fingers trembling as he tried to load the gun. He'd put it there for safety, but he never expected he would need to use it.

Nothing like this was supposed to happen to his family. They were good, church-going people. God was supposed to protect them. But it didn't feel like anybody was protecting them right now.

Where are you, Lord?

He leaned against the wall as his heart raced and he tried to catch his breath. He didn't think he was brave enough to face down the monster in the kitchen. Even thinking about it made his legs weak.

He could just slide down the wall to the floor and pull the door shut. He could hide until the danger was past, but as tempting as it was to hide, it was up to him to save what was left of his family.

A woman's cry cut through the shock of his thoughts, jarring him into action. He stumbled out of the closet, following the sounds of a struggle down the hall into the kitchen, where he froze with his finger on the trigger of the rifle.

The man who had broken into his home had an arm around Martha's neck, and she was gasping for breath between her tears.

Gus looked from his wife to the man pressing a knife against her pregnant stomach, a man too violent and insane to reason with. A man he hoped he would never see again.

16

Now

Marx stood on the front porch, watching as Darian escorted a handcuffed Alex Martin across the lawn to his unmarked car.

Alex twisted, trying to pull free, but the older detective out-sized him by three or four inches and a good fifty pounds of muscle. "This is bull! That girl attacked me! She's crazy! Look at this cut on my forehead from that stupid basket!"

Marx's fingers tightened on his biceps. He wanted to pound the lowlife into the ground for putting his hands on Holly. An accident was excusable, but he put his hands on her after she specifically requested to be left alone.

Darian was more than happy to haul him down to the station and book him for battery. Unfortunately, Holly wasn't sure if Alex was the man lurking outside the window. She hadn't gotten a detailed look.

But he was the right height, and it was possible he had come over last night to check out the newcomers. He probably heard from the other boys that a cop had moved in. Finding Holly in the kitchen would've been a pleasant surprise.

Alex Martin might not be a known criminal, but he had the makings of a predator. Marx doubted it would be long before he ended up on the sex offender registry. Unless he was stupid enough to come after one of the ladies Marx loved. Then he would end up on a metal slab in the morgue.

Marx waited for Darian to drive off before heading back inside. He followed the sound of Christmas music into the kitchen.

Mama had fitted Holly with one of her cupcake-patterned aprons, and the strings were wrapped around Holly's midsection three times before being tied in a bow at the small of her back.

He wasn't sure what they were making, but Holly dumped every ingredient within her short arm span into the mixing bowl.

"Good heavens, child." Mama caught her before she could dump the last cup of flour into the bowl. "There are steps to a recipe. We're just mixin' the wet ingredients."

Holly peered into the bowl for a long moment, then looked up at Mama. "The flour's wet now." She switched on the mixer.

Mama laughed and shook her head. "I s'pose, since they're all goin' to the same place, it don't matter much."

Marx leaned against the door frame and smiled as Mama swung to the music, her cheer contagious. Holly tapped along to the music with her foot, trying and failing to find the rhythm.

"Put your hips into it, honey!" Mama hip-bumped her, throwing her off balance.

Holly shot her a frustrated look, then swayed her entire body from side to side in an awkwardly jerky motion.

Marx's laughter carried over the music, and the girls turned in surprise, Holly's cheeks flushing as pink as the cupcake frosting on her apron. "Yes, I saw that."

"Don't embarrass the girl, Ritchie," Mama chided. "She can't help it she got no rhythm."

The problem wasn't that Holly had no rhythm. The problem was that she had spent most of her life trying to remain invisible, avoiding anything that might encourage male attention. She didn't know *how* to relax and move her body. He held out a hand. "Come here, sweet pea."

Holly tilted her head curiously but put down the mixing spoon. She tripped and stumbled over the bunched corner of one of Mama's numerous kitchen rugs along the way and shot it a hateful glare.

He bit back a smile. She was as clumsy-footed as she was kindhearted. When she placed her small, flour-covered hand in his, he couldn't help but wonder—*did her father ever dance with her before he died? Did he twirl her in circles like the little princess she was?*

He closed his fingers over hers and spun her to the length of his arm. She let out a surprised squeak that deteriorated into breathless giggles. He twirled her in the other direction and then back, catching her around the waist and pulling her into a waltz around the kitchen.

Mama clapped. "Oh you remember!"

She had taught him to dance one Christmas eve while they were baking pies to give as gifts. He'd been young at the time, but he remembered dancing through a scented cloud of sweet cinnamon and vanilla.

Holly watched his feet, trying to mirror his steps. He twirled her, and she glided back into position without so much as a stumble. She looked up at him with a beaming smile.

"There you go, you're gettin' it."

This moment—this glow of happiness radiating from Holly—made every moment of dealing with his father worth it. This was what he wanted for her: family, fun, and a place to feel safe and carefree.

17

Now

The warm glow of the bedside candle blurred into streaks of golden light as tiredness clouded Holly's vision.

She lay in bed, snuggled beneath layers of blankets, with her cellphone tucked between her ear and the mountain of pillows.

"I miss you," the voice on the other end of the line said, flooding her stomach with a strange kind of warmth.

She would never have imagined that a man's voice could fill her with such a sense of comfort and longing, but Jordan was different. They had been inseparable as children—partners in mischief—and no matter how far apart they were or what was happening, his voice always reminded her of home.

"How's Riley?" she asked. "Is he being good?"

The bed felt incomplete without her canine companion stretched out beside her. There was so much empty space, and she missed trailing her fingers through his fur as she fell asleep.

"Other than chewing through my jump rope and whining every night because he can't find you, yeah, he's good," Jordan answered, his voice full of the lighthearted amusement she had come to associate with him. "How are things there?"

Holly smiled as she remembered her afternoon in the kitchen with Marx and his mother. "Ms. Martha's teaching me to bake."

"They're keeping the fire extinguisher handy, right?"

She rolled her eyes. "Ha-ha. We made cookies. I guess I kind of did it wrong, but they were still tasty."

"Maybe you can bring some back with you. Along with some pictures."

She glanced at her camera bag on top of the dresser. Photography was her passion, and probably the only thing she was good at—well, that and stumbling into trouble.

Jordan liked to tease her that she could find trouble in an abandoned parking lot, which admittedly wasn't that much of an exaggeration. There was that one time in an abandoned junkyard lot with some gang members and a homeless woman . . .

"I could use some more photos to brighten up my apartment," Jordan said.

"You could use some more furniture to brighten up your apartment."

"Hey," he said with feigned indignation. "I bought a rug while you were gone."

"Like a big area rug for the living room?"

"It's more of a doormat."

Holly let out a tired laugh. "Okay, I'll take some more pictures for you."

After some pestering on his part, she had finally let him view her digital album, and he had started pointing out pictures that he wanted prints of. A part of her wondered if he was just humoring her out of friendship, but she was good enough to make a living at it for several years.

"You staying out of trouble?" he asked, and she bit her bottom lip. She had been hoping he wouldn't ask that question. When she took too long contemplating how to answer, he said, "Your silence is not comforting. What happened?"

She could imagine the concern in his crystalline blue eyes as he waited for her to explain. He was strangely protective of her.

"Um, I sort of had a disagreement with the neighbor, but everyone's fine, so there's nothing to worry about."

"What kind of disagreement? Do I need to come down to Georgia and beat some sense into someone?"

Nope, already did that. "I told you everyone's fine, okay?"

Jordan's frustrated sigh filtered down the line and Holly decided it would be a good idea to change the subject.

"They have chickens. They're so cute. I tried to catch one, but they're fast for having such short legs."

Jordan laughed. "I can't imagine you chasing chickens around the yard. Why were you trying to catch one?"

She yawned. "To pet it." She rubbed a hand over her eyes. "They look so soft."

"Do you remember that old lady two houses down from yours when we were kids? The one with painted eyebrows. Didn't she have a pet chicken?"

"Mmm hmm," Holly said on a yawn. "And a duck named Quacker."

"You sound tired. You want me to hang up so you can sleep?"

"No, keep talking."

She listened to him reminisce about the pets from their childhood neighborhood until she finally drifted to sleep.

Morning sunlight filtered through the maroon drapes, and Holly stretched in the warm bed. It had been a while since she slept that soundly; she hadn't even heard Mr. Gus snoring.

She pushed back the blankets and stood, catching her reflection in the small mirror that hung on the guestroom wall.

Yikes, she thought. *I look like a hedgehog.*

She tried to smooth down her wild hair, but it sprung back up with a life of its own. She twisted it into a messy bun on top of her head and banded it in place.

The sound of raised voices pulled her to the window, and she brushed aside the drapes to peer out.

Marx and his parents gathered around the shed, a structure so warped and crooked that she could probably blow it over with a puff of breath. Her curiosity gave way to concern when Detective Darian strode into view.

What was he doing back?

She changed quickly, tugged on her purple rain boots, and grabbed her camera bag off the dresser before hurrying down the steps. Cold air washed over her the moment she stepped outside, and she shivered.

"I'm tellin' you it was that Martin boy!" Mr. Gus announced, flinging an arm toward Alex Martin's house. "This is his doin'."

"The only problem with that theory is that Alex Martin is still behind bars," Darian explained. "He couldn't have done this."

Holly's eyes widened when she saw the message spray painted across the side of the shed in thick black letters: pig lovers.

Since Mr. Gus and Ms. Martha didn't have any pigs, the message must have been meant as an insult toward law enforcement. Toward Marx.

Marx folded his arms. "This strikes me as somethin' kids would do. They don't have much respect for law enforcement."

"They know you're a cop?" Darian asked.

"He has cop face," Holly chimed in. People could usually take one look at his I-wanna-smash-your-face-off-the-hood-of-my-car expression and deduce that he was a cop. And his first night here, he had confronted the kids hanging out at the neighbor's house. "You didn't . . . smash anyone's face off the hood of a car, did you?"

Marx's lips twitched with amusement. "Not last night."

"You wouldn't believe how many doors I've had slammed in my face 'cause I'm a cop," Darian added. "Parents are as bad as the kids."

"They all need a good whippin', if you ask me," Mr. Gus grumbled.

Holly shot him a dark look. She didn't know all the details, but Marx had told her his dad was an abusive alcoholic.

Mr. Gus noticed the expression on her face and clarified, "I'm talkin' about discipline, not abuse."

"Not that you would know the difference," Marx said under his breath.

"That's enough you two," Ms. Martha admonished, and Damian cleared his throat.

"I been here four times in the past three months, more, if we're talkin' about the neighborhood itself. It's possible some of the local kids targeted you for that reason. What we do know is that Mr. Martin, unpleasant as he may be, ain't responsible for this. That also makes me question whether he had anythin' to do with the other incidents."

"When's he gonna get out?" Holly asked, concerned that he might retaliate against Marx's family for being arrested.

Darian checked his watch. "If he's lucky, by this afternoon. But don't worry. I had a nice long talk with him on the way to lock-up, and somethin' tells me he's gonna keep his hands to himself for the foreseeable future."

Marx wrapped an arm around Holly's shoulders, pulling her close. "Good. I wouldn't wanna have to break his fingers."

Holly leaned into his embrace, both because she loved him and because she forgot her coat and needed to steal some body heat before she started shivering. "So how are you gonna find out who did this to the shed?"

"I'm gonna knock on some doors, see if anybody's willin' to talk. Unfortunately, there's not much else I can do at this point."

Mr. Gus grunted. "Typical."

Darian let the remark roll off him as he fished his cellphone from his pocket. "I do wanna get a picture of the message to show around, and then you can paint over it if you like."

"I can take the picture," Holly offered, pulling the camera from her bag. "My camera's, um . . . better."

Darian scratched the thin strip of beard below his bottom lip. "If you can email it to me, I don't mind at all."

She smiled up at Marx, thrilled to be able to help, and went over to take pictures.

"I s'pose I gotta drag the paint out of the shed and cover this mess up," Mr. Gus grumbled sourly.

Holly captured one last photo, then tucked her camera back into the bag. "I like to paint. I'll help."

"I don't want your help."

She ignored his protests and dashed inside to change into her khaki overalls and sneakers.

18

Now

Several coats of white paint reduced the black letters to pale shadows. One more layer probably would've erased them entirely, but the can of paint was empty.

Gus sent Holly inside to clean up before he put away the supplies. The girl had gotten more paint on herself than on the building. He had never met someone so uncoordinated.

He had been a little concerned when she dragged two cement blocks over from behind the shed, stacked them, and used them as a stepping stool to extend her reach. He'd watched her out of the corner of his vision to make sure she didn't topple over.

The first thing she did was paint a huge smiley face on the side of the shed. When he scolded her for being childish, she added fangs and angry eyebrows.

They didn't speak much, but she sang Christmas songs under her breath. She was a little off key and she didn't know most of the words, but her voice was sweet enough that it didn't bother him. But when she botched the lyrics of "We Three Kings," he corrected her.

"*Moor* and mountain, not *moron* mountain. There weren't any morons in We Three Kings . . . that we know of."

Her cheeks brightened with embarrassment, making her appear even younger than he suspected she was, and she switched to humming instead. Although they said very little to one another, the afternoon left him with a better understanding of why his son adored her.

He snapped the padlock into place over the door latch, securing the shed, and wiped his hands off on a scrap of cloth. The building was almost back to normal, which according to Holly, was bland and boring. She suggested that he paint it purple.

"What kind of man paints his shed purple?" he muttered to himself as he walked back to the house. *Probably the same kind of man who puts cream and sugar in his coffee.* That was one way to ruin a perfectly fine cup of coffee.

Richard sat on the porch steps, eating one of Martha's Christmas tree cookies. He had offered to help with the shed, but unlike Holly—who refused to take no for an answer—he let the matter drop when Gus told him he didn't want his help.

He'd settled for sitting on the porch and watching them work as if he didn't trust Gus to be alone with the girl.

115

As he approached the house, something Holly said while they were painting nagged at the back of Gus's mind.

"Do you love your son?"

"What kind of ignorant question is that? Of course I love my son."

But it was her response rather than her question that slid between his ribs like a knife, piercing his heart: *"I don't think he knows."*

19

Then

Between the rainwater saturating his clothes and the sweat gathering on his palms, the rifle grew slippery in Gus's grip.

A part of him—a dark seed that had been planted years ago—wanted to pull the trigger and bring an end to the man holding his wife hostage. That darkness inside of him held no mercy and no regret.

It had been growing in his soul since he was a child, and it wanted to lash out and destroy everything.

It terrified him.

If not for Martha's love and devotion, he would've lost himself to that darkness years ago. She had given him hope for a better life, a life of love and family. Of grace and forgiveness.

His arms shook as he aimed the gun at the man who was threatening to take it all away. "I told you, I don't know where she went."

"Lies." He swayed on his feet, either because he was drunk beyond reason or because he had a concussion from the gash dripping blood down his forehead. "You always was a worthless liar."

Gus's finger flexed on the trigger, but the knife was too close to Martha's stomach. "I swear I don't know. Please, you don't gotta hurt Martha. You don't gotta hurt our child."

"Probably ain't even your child. These cows sleep anywhere there's a bed."

Martha was nine months pregnant—due any day now with their second child—and there wasn't a doubt in Gus's mind that the baby was his. Martha was the best thing in his life, the first person to ever really love him.

"Gus . . ." Martha gasped, drawing his eyes to hers. "C-Cressy. Where . . ." She must have seen their daughter's fate in his expression, because she began to sob uncontrollably.

Gus's attention dropped back to the knife, which pressed even more deeply into her heaving stomach. "Please. I told you I don't know where Caroline is. What else do you want?"

"I'll find that fat cow and put her down, like I should've done when I found out about you. Put you all down."

The man thrust the blade into Martha's stomach, and Gus's world shattered around him.

20

Now

Martha stood in front of the stove, an apron tied around her waist, and her hair knotted into a bun at the crown of her head with wisps of silvery curls hanging down by her ears.

Gus slipped his arms around her waist from behind and rested the side of his face against hers, savoring the warmth and softness of her skin.

"Gus?" she said, concern in her voice.

He was grateful beyond words that he hadn't lost her all those years ago, in this very kitchen. He had laid new flooring, painted the cabinets, and recovered the countertops with different laminate.

He had done everything in his power to erase that night, even drinking until he blacked out, but he never forgot a single detail.

"I keep thinkin' about that night," he said. "About you, about Cressy."

She turned in his arms to face him. "Gus, what happened that night . . . it's done. And it ain't never gonna happen again."

He wasn't so certain of that. "Detective Darian said there have been a lot of burglaries lately. What if somebody breaks in?"

She cupped his face. "I understand your fear, but a robber just wants things. He ain't here to start a fight or hurt nobody. Besides, if somebody breaks in, I got two strong men to back me up."

He pressed his forehead against hers. "I couldn't protect you last time. I couldn't protect any of you."

"You been holdin' onto that pain for so long that it's rooted in your soul," Martha said softly. "Let it go, Gus. Let the past go."

His throat tightened. "I don't know how."

She draped her arms around his neck, wrapping him in more love and understanding than he deserved. "You need to give it to the Lord. It won't weigh Him down."

Gus clung to Martha's words as he unlocked the side door to the garage and pushed it open. If he was going to let the past go, then it started here.

He fidgeted with the keys as he stared at the old truck parked in the center of the space. He had tried to erase it from his thoughts, like everything else from that night, but hiding it away only seemed to give it the power to haunt him.

He lingered on the raised threshold for a moment before forcing himself to move closer.

A few tugs on the tarp sent it fluttering to the floor at his feet, revealing the dark green truck that he had worked so hard to afford.

He brushed a hand over the bed, bittersweet memories nipping at his fingers. He took Martha out for their first date in this truck. But his last memories were the sharpest—spinning out of control in the rain, the sickening thump as he hit their baby girl . . .

And the gun he'd hidden away in the back. Feeling the dusty surface of his old rifle brought that night flooding back with excruciating clarity.

The gunshot resounded through the kitchen, and a stain spread across the intruder's chest. He staggered, eyes wide with disbelief, and collapsed to the floor in slow motion.

Gus's heart slammed against his ribs as he kept the barrel pointed at the prone man, the Christian in him horrified of what he had just done, and the darkness inside him roaring in triumph.

Gus wrenched his hand back from the rifle. He couldn't do this. Confronting it was too much. Unless he had a little something to calm his nerves. His gaze trailed to the lock box on the shelf by the tool chest.

Temptation pulled him toward it, and he opened the box, reaching in for the bottle of beer he kept for emergencies. It felt at home in his hand, smooth and heavy, and comfortingly familiar.

"Lord, I want it." So badly that he could taste it. "But . . . I don't want it."

He gazed at the bottle as conflicting urges warred inside him. Alcohol soothed the pain, at least for a little while, but he couldn't break his promise to Martha. The bottle slipped in his grip when the side garage door opened, and he barely managed to catch it.

Richard appeared in the doorway, anger tightening his features. "Why am I not surprised to find you with a bottle of alcohol?"

Gus swallowed, guilt crawling through his stomach. "It ain't what you think."

"If you wanna drink yourself into a heart attack, go right ahead. But at least be honest about it with Mama." Richard shook his head and turned to leave, his voice drifting back over his shoulder. "Dinner's ready."

Gus sank onto the workbench and stared at the bottle. The disgust in Richard's voice made him want to twist the cap off and pour it down the drain. But he just couldn't seem to do it.

A quiet tap on the door drew his head up. Holly stood in the grass outside and peered around the edge of the door frame, her large hat slipping down over her eyes.

She pushed it back. "Are you okay, Mr. Gus?"

"What do you want?"

"I saw you and Marx arguing, so I thought I would see if you were okay." She stepped inside. "You don't look okay."

He didn't have the patience to deal with her right now, and it came through in the sharpness of his tone. "Did I say I wanted company?"

She meandered into the garage, her brown eyes traveling the walls. "You didn't say you didn't."

"Well I don't."

Either she was too daft to understand, or she chose to ignore the fact that he didn't want her company. She ran a gloved hand over the side of his truck. "Pretty."

He stood, his anger rising with him, and slammed the bottle onto the work table behind him. "Don't touch that!"

Holly cringed as his deep voice thundered around the garage. But she didn't scurry back outside in a panic the way he expected; instead, she straightened her shoulders and glared at him. "If you don't want me to touch it, fine, but you don't have to yell."

He dropped back onto the bench with a sigh, and her boots scraped the cement floor with every step as she crossed the garage to join him. "You know, for somebody with such tiny feet, you walk like they're weighted down by cement blocks."

She perched on the far side of the bench and stretched her feet out in front of her. "My feet aren't that small."

"My big toe is longer than your foot."

She let out a tiny squeak of amusement and pulled off one of her purple boots, offering it to him.

"What am I supposed to do with your shoe?"

"Try it on. I'm calling your bluff."

"I am not tryin' on a girl's purple boot covered in sparkles. Put that thing back on."

Her lips curled into a smirk as she tugged the boot back on over her striped fuzzy sock. She dropped her feet to the floor and then pawed around in the pocket of her coat. She pulled out a wadded napkin decorated with poinsettias, unwrapped it, and picked a piece of hard tac candy.

"I stole some sweets." She popped a cherry one into her mouth and held up her hand in offering. "Want one? I'm pretty sure they taste better than that." She nodded toward the beer. "The cherry ones anyway."

He grimaced at her. "Do you make a habit of gettin' on people's nerves?"

"Do you make a habit of being a grouch?"

"I am not a grouch."

"Your eyebrows disagree."

He tried to smooth the irritation from his expression and chose a piece of black licorice from her palm. She wrinkled her nose, but he enjoyed a bitter edge to his candy. They sucked on their candy in silence, but he could feel her watching him. "Either say what's on your mind or—"

"Marx said you stopped drinking." She pushed the candy into her cheek so it didn't slur her speech when she spoke again. "So why the bottle?"

"You wouldn't understand."

"I might."

This girl, with her sparkly boots and fuzzy socks couldn't possibly know how it felt to take a life. "Have you ever killed somebody?"

She shook her head.

"Then you can't understand."

She scraped the bottoms of her boots on the floor as she stared at her knees, and the repetitive sound made him want to throw them across the room. "So . . . can I ask you a question, Mr. Gus?"

Lord have mercy. She was going to drive him insane. "Don't ask if you can ask me a question, girl. Just ask the question."

"People don't usually become alcoholics because they enjoy the taste. Are you . . . trying not to think about something?"

"Do you drink?"

"No."

"Then what could you possibly know about it?"

She shrugged her shoulders, her attention still fixed on her knees. "When I was thirteen, I had a foster dad who was an alcoholic. About four or five beers in, he would get angry and start looking for somebody to hurt."

Lines creased her forehead, as though the memory troubled her.

"He would get angry about the strangest things. *Little* things. Like one of us not turning off the faucet all the way or forgetting to put our shoes in the closet."

He clenched his teeth against the words he wanted to say. Boys needed a firm hand, but girls were to be treated with gentleness. They were smaller and more delicate, and the idea of a grown man knocking around a thirteen year old girl for forgetting to turn off a faucet made him want to return the favor.

He had been firm with Richard from the moment he learned to talk, but he had never once considered laying a harsh hand on Cressy.

"I don't think my foster dad was a bad man," Holly said, toying with the bracelet on her wrist. "I think he was hurting. But when he drank to forget his pain, he also forgot who he was. And there was so much anger inside him that it just . . . erupted."

Something about her words struck him deeper than they should have, as though she were talking about him rather than her foster dad. But he had never abused his children.

"Sometimes he didn't even remember giving his wife a black eye or leaving bruises on one of the kids. I never knew if it was because he drank so much he couldn't remember, or that he just didn't *wanna* remember."

Fragments of voices and images stirred in the back of his mind, so hazy that they could've been bits and pieces of a bad dream.

A child screaming and sobbing as he dragged him out from underneath the kitchen sink. "It's for your own good!"

The belt in his hand snapping down.

Gus jerked as if the belt had struck him, and his hand fell to the buckle beneath his belly button. No, it had to be a dream. A nightmare. He would never have beaten his son like that.

But he vaguely remembered Richard, maybe eight years old, walking stiffly through the house as though every part of his body hurt. He'd taken off when Gus asked him what was wrong, and Gus had been too far gone to notice when he came back.

Rage darkened his vision and he swung out, backhanding someone across the face. "You are a worthless waste of time!"

"No, I didn't. I didn't do that to my son. I wouldn't." Gus released a shuddering breath as the fragmented memories pelted him one after another.

Martha screaming at him to stop.

Richard gazing up at him from the floor with fear and anger in his eyes.

His own voice shouting as he folded his belt in his hand. "I'll give you somethin' to cry about!"

"What did I tell you about bein' more careful! Clumsy idiot!"

Tears blurred his vision and he struggled to breathe as Holly's words pounded against him like fists: *sometimes he didn't even remember leaving bruises on one of the kids.*

What had he done? All those nights he drank just to forget his own pain, bottle after bottle until he blacked out. What had he done to his family?

"Mr. Gus." Holly touched his shoulder, her voice so soft that he could barely hear it over his own heart cracking to pieces.

He'd known there was a darkness inside of him, but he still drank until he disappeared, leaving nothing and no one to stand between that darkness and his family. It was a wonder he hadn't hurt Martha, too.

He slapped the unopened bottle of beer off the counter and it shattered on the cement, the liquid poison spreading across the floor.

Holly leaped to her feet, backing away from his anger, but he couldn't bring himself to care. He leaned his elbows on his knees and pressed his face into his hands, his shoulders shaking as he fought back tears.

He had become the thing he feared most—the monster his son believed him to be. Martha was right. He *had* driven their son away.

"Lord, what have I done?"

A tentative hand touched his shoulder, giving it a gentle pat as if it might soothe the gaping wound that had opened up where his heart used to be. "You're not a bad person, Mr. Gus. You've done bad things, but you're not a bad person."

Gus rubbed the dampness from his face and looked up at her, her eyes shining with compassion. "I don't think my son would agree with you."

She sat back down beside him. "I don't know. But I do know that he's here now, and you have a chance to make amends."

The liquid on the floor trickled toward the drain, like his life, and he shook his head. "Richard will never forgive me."

"You don't know that."

"I know——" He bit off the words. He started to say that he knew his son, but it would be a lie.

When Richard left at eighteen, Gus had been certain his boy was slipping down the same slope of sin and infidelity. So much so that he didn't bother keeping up on Richard's career or personal life. He avoided all of it because he couldn't bear the disappointment or the reminder that he had failed as a father. Apart from some shared physical features and a volatile temperament, his son was a stranger.

"I know that if I was him, I wouldn't forgive me."

"Marx isn't you. He's made his own mistakes, but he has one of the biggest hearts. I have nothing to offer him, but he loves me anyway. He's risked his life for mine. You don't know the man I know."

"Would you forgive your foster father for what he did?"

"Yes."

He sighed, too tired and too heartbroken to argue anymore. He held out his hand. "Give me one of them candies." When she placed another licorice candy in his palm, he tossed it into his mouth.

"Will you try to talk to Marx? Please?"

Her expression was strategically cute, one of those things women could do with their faces to convince a man to jump off a cliff for her. "If you stop tryin' to bewitch me with your face, yes, I'll talk to him."

To his surprise, she threw her arms around his neck and hugged him. He hesitated, then tapped her back awkwardly until she released him.

21

Now

Marx admired the Christmas lights twinkling in the distance as he sat on the porch swing. Every house in the neighborhood was different: some simple and classic with white lights, others wildly colorful, and some wreathed in blinking atrocities that made him thankful he wasn't epileptic.

He lifted a mug of coffee to his lips and savored the warmth that trickled down his throat. He didn't usually drink caffeine this late, but he had no intention of sleeping. He wanted to make sure nothing more happened to his parents' house or property.

A shadow moved in the pool of light spilling onto the porch from inside the house, and he found his father standing in the doorway.

Just what I need.

Dad, bundled in a flannel jacket, joined him on the porch. He cleared his throat. "I was hopin' we could talk."

"You can talk until you're hoarse, for all I care, but don't expect me to listen."

Dad sat down in the chair in front of the living room window and rubbed his hands together. "There's some things we need to discuss."

"I have nothin' to discuss with you. You know nothin' about me or my life."

"You're right. I been makin' assumptions about you 'cause I expected you to make the same mistakes I did."

"Is that your idea of an apology?"

"No, it's the beginnin' of an explanation." He picked nervously at the callouses on his hands with his short fingernails. "I never wanted to be my father, but somehow . . . well, somehow I ended up a lot like him."

"I wouldn't know. Never met the man. You and Mama never talked about him or Grandma. I just assumed they were dead."

"Your grandmother died givin' birth to me. I don't think Daddy ever forgave me for that, for takin' away the one person he claimed to love. He made sure I knew every day that I was the reason he hated his life."

"Made sure you knew how?"

Dad drew in a fortifying breath and stood, stripping out of his flannel jacket. With shaking fingers, he began to unbutton his shirt. "I don't mean this to be an excuse, 'cause it ain't. But you deserve to know." He pulled his arms free and turned, baring his back.

Marx nearly dropped his coffee mug. Pale, thin scars stretched across his father's back like feathers. He swallowed the bile that crept up his throat. "He did that to you?"

His father redressed slowly, as if the old wounds still ached, and sat back down. "It got worse as I got older. I thought for sure he was gonna kill me one day, so I ran away just before I turned eighteen."

Marx couldn't find the words to respond. All these years and he'd never known the horrors of his own dad's childhood. He'd never asked.

"I found a job at a textile mill. A couple years later, I met your mama. She was easily the prettiest girl I ever seen. I asked her to marry me not five months later, and I about fell over when she said yes." A rueful smile curled his lips. "I think she might've been the first person to ever love me."

Marx leaned forward, listening. He had never been offered this window into the past, and as much as he wanted to be indifferent, he couldn't help but be drawn in.

"Shortly after we moved here, we found out she was pregnant with your sister, Cressy, and for the first time in my life, I was happy. But I should've known better. There was no escapin' where I came from."

Dad rubbed his hands together and stared out across the yard, regret and pain deepening the wrinkles in his forehead. Unease churned in Marx's gut as he waited for him to explain.

"My daddy remarried when I was fifteen. I guess it didn't take her but a few years to realize the mess she'd gotten herself into. I didn't keep in touch with either of 'em, so I didn't even know she'd left him. All I know is, your mama and me had three years of peace before it all started."

"What started? What happened?"

Dad sighed and looked down at his hands. "It started with shoe prints in the grass, a man's face peerin' in the windows. I didn't see him, but your mama did."

That was why Dad had looked so shaken when Marx told him Holly saw a face outside of the window. Why not just explain it when he asked?

"And then . . . I was drivin' home late and it was rainin'. And your sister, she was just . . . standin' there in the middle of the road. I tried to stop."

"You hit Cressy?"

He nodded solemnly. "I thought she was dead. She *should've* been dead. She was so still and lifeless when I carried her body up to the house, but somehow . . . she survived."

Marx's mind drifted back in time to a night when he crawled into his big sister's bed and cuddled against her, offering his Teddy bear for comfort. She barely noticed he was there as she cried, terrified of the rain pattering against the windows.

Cressy could never explain why rainstorms after dark made her anxious. She'd been too young to remember the details when the accident happened, but

her mind had still made a connection between the rain
that sent their father's car spinning out of control and
the fear she must have felt just before the impact.

"The accident is why she has the limp, isn't it?"
Marx asked. He and Cressy used to dream up wild stories
for how she'd gotten it: jumping out of a plane without
a parachute, getting attacked by leg-stealing pirates, or
accidentally stepping in a hole in the yard where the little
gophers would nibble off part of your leg and most of
your toes.

"The doctors had to remove part of the bone
'cause it was shattered, and it just never healed right."

"Why was she in the middle of the road? Where
was Mama?"

Mama was far too protective of her children to
ever let them out of her sight for long. She wouldn't have
just let Cressy run around outside in the rain by herself.

"When I carried Cressy up to the house, I
realized somebody had broke in. The door was wide
open, and she had just . . . wandered out."

Marx stared at him in horror. "Who? Who broke
into the house?"

"My father."

After everything Marx had just learned about his
grandfather—the anger, the brutality—his stomach
crawled with dread. "Did he hurt Mama?"

"Caroline left him and he was convinced that I
knew where she was hidin', but I—"

Marx slammed his coffee mug down on the
porch railing. He couldn't care less about Caroline. His

only concern was for his mother and his sister. "Did he *hurt* Mama?!"

His father struggled to rein in the grief and anger pouring out of him with every detail. "He stabbed her in the stomach. I think he meant to take you both from me, but the doctors were able to do an emergency c-section."

Marx stared at him as he tried to absorb his meaning. "You're tellin' me he stabbed Mama in the stomach while she was pregnant with me?"

"I don't know how, but . . . the blade missed you. Not even a scratch. I couldn't explain it; neither could the doctors."

Marx scrubbed his hands over his face and leaned back in the swing, staring up at the ceiling. He hoped his grandfather was dead, because if he wasn't, he was more than willing to fix that problem. "Where is he now? My grandfather."

"Cemetery down the road." Dad rubbed at his swollen knuckles, his expression troubled. "I shot him that night."

As the gravity of his dad's words slowly sank in, Marx bowed his head. All these years, Dad had been living with the weight of killing his own father.

As a cop, Marx had been forced to end more lives than he cared to think about. And regardless of the circumstances, every human life he took chipped away another little piece of his soul.

God would forgive him, but Marx would remember every face and every name until the day he died.

"I'm sorry you had to do that," he said, looking over at his dad. "But he didn't give you a choice. You did what you had to do to protect your family."

Conflicting emotions clouded his eyes, and he looked away. "I don't know. A part of me regrets pullin' that trigger, but the other part of me . . . is glad he's dead."

"It's normal to feel regret for takin' a life, Dad. And it's okay to be relieved that it's over."

"But it ain't over." Dad stood and paced the porch, agitation fueling his steps. "Every time I think about that night, I see my father standin' in our kitchen completely unarmed, my gun pointed at his chest."

Marx let out a long breath as he absorbed the meaning behind his words. His grandfather must have lost the knife after stabbing Mama, which left him defenseless. Dad pulled the trigger anyway.

"He would've gone after you next, and likely would've come back to finish off Mama. After everythin' he did, he wasn't just gonna lay down on the floor in surrender. You had every reason to fear for your life and our family."

And no court of law would convict his father for choosing to pull that trigger. Had Marx been in his father's shoes, he probably would've made the same decision.

"I tried to erase that night from existence." Dad collapsed back into the chair, as if the confession had sapped the strength from his legs. "I drank until I couldn't remember my own name."

Marx had gotten some of the worst beatings in his life on those nights. But unlike his dad, he remembered them in the morning. Dad would wake up with a hangover and no recollection of why his knuckles were raw.

When people drank themselves into a mindless stupor, they did things they wouldn't ordinarily do. Marx could understand why Dad would lose his mind every time he was wasted. But he was an angry man even when he was sober.

There were mornings when Dad hadn't so much as smelled a beer, and he still pulled off his belt to whip Marx for everything—for lying when he was telling the truth, for breaking a glass when he tripped up the steps, for forgetting to pray before eating.

That was the man he hated. The man who could control his decisions and still chose to hurt him.

"When I pulled the trigger that night, I became a man who . . . murdered his enemy, abandoned his family for alcohol, and cheated on his wife," Dad said, his voice thick with regret. "I was desperate to forget what I had done and to find somethin' or somebody to fill that void."

Marx sat back in the swing and folded his arms, his tone flat and indifferent. "Well I hope you found what you were lookin' for."

"I'm sorry, Richard."

"For what? For cheatin' on Mama? For drinkin' until you beat me senseless? What about all the times when you were sober? Like when you whipped me for cheatin' on a test at school, or because I was afraid of the dark. Are you sorry for that, too?"

Dad opened his mouth, sputtering. "I don't . . ."

"Don't remember? I was maybe six, and I cried because you turned off my bedroom light and closed the door, and Mama never did that. Do you remember what you said when you came back into my room with your belt?" Marx paused to give his dad time to answer, but he didn't. "'I'll give you somethin' to cry about.' Well you succeeded. I stopped fearin' the darkness, because I realized that the only monster I needed to fear . . . was you."

Dad flinched. "I don't remember doin' that."

"Of course you don't. You whipped me so much that I can't even remember every time it happened or what it was for. You wanna apologize for bein' a drunk philanderer, that's fine, but you—sober you—that's the man I will never forgive."

Tears pooled in his dad's eyes and spilled down his face. "I didn't realize . . . I thought I was makin' you a better man than me. A better man than my father."

"You thought wrong. But luckily, I turned out just fine in spite of you."

Dad gazed at him, and for the first time, Marx could see through his father's hardened shell to the vulnerable and broken man beneath. A man with forty-eight years of guilt slowly crushing his spirit.

"I never meant to become like my father, but the darkness he planted in me when I was a boy—the anger, the hatred—"

"He treated you the way no human bein' should be treated, but that's not an excuse for the choices you made."

"I raised you the only way I knew how. I . . . I didn't know how else to be."

Marx leaned forward, meeting his dad's eyes. "You raised me to be angry and bitter, to punish people weaker than me when they make a mistake or do somethin' I don't like, to bully people in to doin' things my way. But I had a choice too, Dad, and I chose not to be like you."

Dad swallowed. "I realize now that I did things wrong, but I can't change them. I just hope that . . . someday you can forgive me."

22

Now

The night passed uneventfully, but Marx had enough on his mind to keep him awake as the hours crept by.

He couldn't shake the image of the scars on his dad's back. To be a child, trapped alone in a house with a raging, violent alcoholic . . . the fear that must have haunted every moment.

There were mornings when he used to creep out of the house on his toes, trying to escape into the outdoors before the angry monster woke.

Had Dad done the same when he was younger? When he was just a scared little boy in need of a safe place to disappear?

It was hard to imagine his father as a child, little Gus, just trying to survive the nightmare that was his everyday life. There had been no one to protect him.

Marx had Mama to soothe and comfort him, and a big sister to deflect Dad's anger. There were times when the only reason Marx didn't get backhanded across the room was because Cressy shielded him by stepping between him and Dad.

She'd taken a stand against violence even then, when they were just children, and now she spent her life protecting women and children against violence in the home. Dad had never laid a hand on her, but she had witnessed more than enough to inspire her to action.

It would've been easier to surrender to the cycle of violence than to stand against it. Abuse becomes an instinctive way of life, anger and violence passed down through generations. But all it takes is one person to stand up and say, "Enough."

Cressy became a social worker and Marx became a cop, both of them not only determined to end that cycle of violence with their father, but intent on seeking justice for others.

Holly shuffled out a few minutes before dawn, bringing a blanket and two mugs of hot chocolate with her. She didn't say a word as she curled up on the swing next to him.

The radish-pink tip of her nose told him that she had been crying. He considered asking if she wanted to talk about what was bothering her, but given the hour, it was likely a nightmare.

He wrapped an arm around her and they watched the sun rise over steaming mugs of hot cocoa.

He sipped the cup of molten marshmallow hot chocolate and nearly choked. Good grief. It tasted like diabetes in a cup. What in the world had she done to it?

She tipped her head back to look up at him. "I added hot fudge to make it extra chocolatey. Do you like it?"

He forced himself to swallow and then washed it down with the cold coffee on the railing. "It's very . . . sweet."

"I like it."

"Of course you do. You're addicted to . . ." He caught himself before the word slipped out, but it was too late.

Holly's eyes danced with mischief and she snuggled closer, making him laugh.

Every now and then, she called him Sugar simply because she knew it unnerved him. Mama could call him Sugar, his wife or girlfriend could call him Sugar, but it didn't sound right coming from the little peanut he thought of as a daughter.

"I could call you Ritchie," she said, but her nose crinkled the moment the name left her lips. "That sounds weird."

Marx laughed again. She had never called him by his first name or any variation thereof, and it probably felt as strange to her as calling her *Ms. Cross* would to him.

"You can call me whatever you want. Just don't call me Sugar."

"Okay, Donald."

He laughed, realizing she was trying to guess his middle name. "My middle name is not Donald."

"Dan?" She straightened. "Gimme a clue."

"Sure. It starts with D."

She rolled her eyes and heaved a dramatic sigh as she slumped back down against him.

The slam of a car door drew his attention to a taxi down the street. The tail lights flashed before it drove off, leaving Alex Martin standing in an orange pool of light from the overhead street lamp.

The mere sight of him rekindled the fire in Marx's veins, and if Holly weren't cuddled up next to him, he would march over there to remind him why keeping his hands to himself was better for his health.

Alex looked toward them, shouted a few crude suggestions, and stalked up the sidewalk to his house.

Marx shook his head and lifted the coffee mug to take another drink, forgetting that it wasn't coffee until he convulsively spat sickeningly sweet hot chocolate back into the mug. He set the dreadful concoction aside so he didn't make that mistake again.

Holly yawned and then leaned more heavily against him, her body relaxing. "Only a few days until Christmas."

He smiled and brushed a strand of hair back from her face. "Maybe later we'll do some Christmas shoppin'."

"I like that idea. What do you want for Christmas?"

It was such a simple question, but nothing he longed for could be wrapped in a gift box and tied with a bow. It certainly wouldn't fit beneath a tree. "I'm a bit old for Christmas."

"You're a bit old for *Santa* who, let's be honest, is kind of creepy when you really think about it."

"How so?"

"Anybody else who stalks children and breaks into their houses at night is probably gonna get arrested."

He snorted in amusement. "I think you've spent too much time around cops."

She grinned. "Maybe. But you're never too old to celebrate the birth of Jesus with your family."

"I suppose." He rested his head back against the swing and watched the clouds roll by. He had always loved Christmas. The gifts and decorations were sparse in their house growing up, but it was the one day each year that his dad had been consistently sober.

On Christmas day, he could almost believe that his father loved him. But the day came and went, and before darkness fell, his dad had a beer in his hand and anger in his eyes.

Holly pressed something small and round into his palm before pulling her hand back, and he gazed at it curiously. "What's this for?"

"Your thoughts."

"The expression is a *penny* for your thoughts, Holly. Not a nickel."

She scooted upright on the swing. "I figured I would skip the whole negotiating thing and get right to the sharing of your thoughts. That and, I didn't have a penny, so . . ." She looked at him expectantly. "What's bothering you?"

"What makes you think somethin's botherin' me?"

"I can see it." She touched the skin just above his nose with light fingers, making him suddenly aware that his troubled thoughts had etched a line between his eyebrows.

He turned the nickel over between his thumb and forefinger as he considered how to answer her question. "I've got a lot on my mind. You, Mama, the upcomin' trial."

"Your dad."

"Mmm hmm. We had a long conversation last night, one that was about thirty-some years overdue."

"How'd it go?"

"He wants me to forgive him." He flicked the coin, watching it fall head over tails until he snatched it out of the air. "I can forgive the drinkin' and the violence it led to. I can even forgive the fact that he cheated on Mama. But he made a conscious decision to make my life miserable. How do I forgive that?"

Most people wouldn't know it by looking at her, but Holly had a stockpile of wisdom and life experience for someone her age. She often answered things in a way he didn't expect.

She stared hard at the swing, her mind turning over the question. "I think . . . sometimes we do things that feel normal to us without really considering how they make someone else feel."

"I don't follow."

"When we met, you were kind of, um . . . rude."

"I was not rude. You, Ms. Holly, were stubborn."

Her lips quirked as she tried to hold back a smile. "I think you're remembering it wrong."

"Mmm hmm. Go on with your point."

"Do you remember when you got . . . really frustrated with me?"

He got frustrated with her frequently, but the hesitation in her voice told him which moment she was talking about. "You mean when I yelled at you in your apartment and scared you."

She squirmed. "I was gonna say *unsettled* me, but yeah, that time. Yelling was kind of normal for you."

He hadn't given much thought to moderating his tone before meeting her. If he was angry, people knew it. Shannon, his ex-wife, was a lawyer with a backbone of steel, and when he shouted in anger, she returned it in kind.

"Did you consider that the way you acted might unsettle me?" Holly asked.

"Honestly, no. It never occurred to me."

"And you didn't realize it until someone pointed it out."

He sighed and squeezed the nickel in his fist. He knew she had forgiven him for that incident, but he still hated that he'd scared her so badly. "I was raised on

C.C. Warrens

anger and explosive tempers. That was normal for me. And I get what you're sayin'—that to my dad, the way he treated me was normal. So much so that he didn't realize how it was affectin' me. But that doesn't make it any easier to forgive him."

"Who told you forgiveness is easy?"

"I guess I just assumed."

"When Izzy asked me for forgiveness, I struggled with it for months."

Isabel Lane. Even thinking the woman's name prickled his temper. She had taken Holly in when she was nine, giving her hope for a family only to decide that drug dealing was more important than the little girl she proclaimed to love. He couldn't stand that woman, and if it were up to him, she would never communicate with Holly again.

"I was so . . . angry with her and so,"—Holly stared off into the distance as she struggled to find her words— "brokenhearted that she didn't choose me, that I wasn't enough."

"Oh, sweetheart." He ran a hand over her hair, wishing he could erase that doubt from her mind.

"It took me a long time to forgive her, and to understand why I needed to."

In Marx's opinion, that murdering drug dealer didn't deserve forgiveness, but Holly had a much kinder heart than he did. She showed compassion to the types of people others went out of their way to avoid.

148

"Holding on to that anger and bitterness toward her . . . it was hurting *me*. It was like I was letting her break my heart over and over, long after she was no longer a part of my life. When our hearts get broken, they need tender care just like any other wound. But hanging on to pain and anger constantly rips the wound open, and eventually a bitter infection settles inside so deeply that it will never heal."

Marx's breath left his lips in a puff of steam as he mulled over her words. It had been thirty years since his father laid a hand on him, but somehow it felt like only yesterday.

"I can't tell you how to handle this issue with your dad, but forgiving Izzy gave both of us a sense of peace." She leaned back against him. "I want that for you."

He hugged her tightly and placed a kiss in her rumpled hair. "What would I do without you, sweet pea?"

"Be really grouchy all the time."

He laughed. "You're probably right."

Holly sniffed the air and straightened, scenting the bacon before he did. "I smell breakfast."

That must mean Mama was awake and preparing a morning meal. "Let's go help with breakfast, and then we'll go shoppin'."

Holly trotted toward the stove with the bowl of pancake mix. It was only a matter of time before she noticed the chocolate chips and marshmallows Mama had pulled out of the cupboard for her.

He saw the moment she caught sight of them, because she looked between the bowl and the bags of goodies, her bottom lip caught between her teeth. He knew she was contemplating dumping them into the batter to make a s'more pancake.

Just when he resigned himself to the fact that he was going to have marshmallows in his pancakes, she decided not to add them to the mix. Instead, she sprinkled them over her pancake in the skillet, poured more batter on top, then patted the pancake with the spatula as if she were trying to flatten it out.

Marx's lips twitched and he looked at Mama, who sat next to him at the table. "I can't believe you're lettin' her cook the pancakes after I warned you. That pancake's gonna weigh five pounds."

"She's doin' fine."

"Just wait till she has to flip it. The only place that pancake's goin' is on the floor."

Holly hummed along to Frosty the Snowman and continued poking at her pancake as if that would somehow make it cook faster.

Mama cocked her head curiously. "Has she never made a pancake before?"

"Those little frozen ones you put in the microwave." At his mother's appalled expression, he explained, "Holly lived most of her life on the run with very little money, so she mostly bought foods that she could shove into a bag and take with her—Pop Tarts, cereal, potato chips. Things like that."

A peculiar look crossed her face. "When I offered her cookies on the porch, I thought it was odd that she put two of 'em in her bag."

"It's a habit. I suppose until she knows for a fact that she doesn't have to run anymore, she'll always have a bag packed and ready to go."

"Well, I'm gonna teach her to cook her food instead of gettin' it out of a package."

"Just don't let her make the coffee."

Holly tried to flip her enormously fat pancake but it plopped halfway out of the skillet. She frantically tried to scoop it back into the pan before the burner could start smoking.

Marx's mother leaned toward him and whispered, "I see what you mean."

Marx chuckled and went to help Holly salvage her breakfast. She loved pancakes, and he had gotten quite good at making them. She frowned at the butchered pancake and looked as though she might start whacking it with the spatula out of frustration.

Marx took the utensil from her before she could do any more damage. "You're tryin' to flip an obese pancake with a tiny flipper. You either need to cut the pancake in half or use two spatulas."

Once he showed her how to properly size and flip a pancake, she was able to prepare a pile of perfectly cooked silver dollar pancakes on her own. She carried the platter of pancakes to the table with pride in her step. To anyone else they might just be pancakes, but to Holly, they were an accomplishment.

Mama finished the eggs and bacon, and he set them on the table just as Dad ambled into the kitchen.

Tension stretched between them when their eyes met, and they mutually decided to ignore one another.

"Morning!" Holly exclaimed, far too chipper for someone who didn't drink caffeine in the morning. She offered his father a mug of decaf coffee.

Dad blinked at her as he accepted it, then asked Marx, "Is she high on somethin'?"

"Just hot chocolate and Jesus." He pulled out a chair for his mother. "Mama."

She smiled as she took a seat. Holly plopped down in her chair before he could do the same for her and offered him a triumphant smile.

She had asked him once if his opening doors and pulling out chairs for women was one of his perplexing male Southernisms, and if she wasn't trying to flip the roles on him, she was trying to beat him to the punch.

"Mmm hmm," he said, no intention of letting her win this little battle. He lifted her chair off the ground, just enough to send her scrambling to grip the edges and moved her closer to the table. He leaned down and whispered into her hair, "Nice try, peanut, but you're not exactly heavy."

Her eyebrows dipped in disapproval, and she muttered something under her breath about peanuts.

"Let's thank the good Lord for this meal." Mama offered a hand to Holly, who hesitated before placing her fingers on top.

Marx made no move to finish the link by taking his father's hand, and neither did his dad.

"You two will settle your differences before God, if only for this prayer, or you will not eat," Mama said firmly.

"Mama—"

"Don't you Mama me, Ritchie. Take your father's hand."

Reluctantly, he did, and they bowed their heads so Mama could pray over the food.

"Heavenly father, thank you for the blessin's you rain down on us. Thank you for my baby comin' home, and for this precious girl you've brought into our lives."

Marx felt the shift in Holly's posture, and he cracked an eye to see the surprise on her face. She wasn't accustomed to being viewed as precious, even though she was precious to him.

"Bless this food to the nourishment of our bodies, and our bodies to Thy service. In Jesus' name. Amen."

They broke apart. Martha began filling the plates and passing them down. She plopped Holly's enormous pancake on a plate, added a few strips of bacon, two biscuits, and scrambled eggs before setting the plate in front of Holly.

Holly's eyes widened. "Ms. Martha, this is—"

"Less talkin', more eatin'. You need to put some meat on them bones or the breeze is apt to blow you away."

Marx choked on his swallow of orange juice at the expression on Holly's face. He'd told her that if she ever met his mother, she would declare her too skinny and completely adorable. And she had just called her precious and bone skinny in the span of five minutes.

Holly slid an accusing look his way as she stabbed a forkful of pancake. "I see where you get it from."

Mama spread jam across her biscuit, a small smile lifting the corners of her lips. "I need to do some last minute Christmas shoppin', and then we'll have some eggnog while we decorate the tree together. Would you like that, Holly?"

Holly brightened. "Absolutely." She dug into her mountain of food, no doubt eager to get it over with so she could go buy Christmas presents and decorate a tree.

23

Now

Holly dragged her bags of gifts from the backseat and dashed toward the house before anyone else was out of the car.

Marx offered Mama a hand out of the backseat, and she smiled up at him. "That girl is such a joy. I can't remember the last time I saw somebody so excited about Christmas."

Holly had brought her camera, snapping photos of every decorated house along the way. When they finally reached the department store, she meandered down every Christmas aisle, gravitating toward glittery ornaments and pre-lit trees with color-changing tips. Every five seconds, he heard her gasp and wander off to look at something else.

He expected his dad to have something rude or negative to say about Holly's joy for Christmas, but he didn't say anything as he climbed out of the passenger's side.

"Marx."

The alarm in Holly's voice snapped his attention toward the front porch, where she stood. He left his gift bags on the hood of the car and crossed the lawn to join her.

Holly still had her hand extended toward the door, which rested against the door frame, unlatched. But he'd seen Mama lock it. He pushed Holly's arm away.

"Back to the car. Stay with my parents. Tell Mama to call the police." He waited for her to retreat before drawing his gun and nudging the door inward a few inches.

It scraped across red and silver glass ornaments, and he stepped carefully as he crept inside. His eyes swept the entryway, glossing over the toppled furniture and broken glass as he searched for an intruder.

He eyed the dark second floor, then climbed the steps one quiet creak at a time, keeping his gun trained on the darkness.

He opened each door, the dim evening light pouring through the windows revealing that each room had been tossed. Holly's suitcase had been dumped on the bed, her clothes strewn across the floor, but the photograph of her family appeared to be untouched.

Thank you, Lord, for small favors.

His parents' room, however, looked like a tornado had ripped through it and then doubled back for another pass. He checked the closet to make sure no one was hiding in it and noticed the gun cabinet.

It was a wooden cabinet with a lock, but the door was made of glass. Pointless. Whoever wanted the guns had simply broken the glass and pulled them out.

How many guns did his dad have?

The sudden squeak of the screen door pulled him back down the hall, and he found his father standing in the foyer. He snapped his gun back down to his side with frustration and descended the steps. "Are you tryin' to get yourself shot?"

Glass crunched beneath Dad's shoes as he moved down the hall with slow, dazed steps. He stopped in the middle of the living room, looking around at the toppled tree and broken decorations. "This wasn't s'posed to happen again."

He bent to pick up a small jewelry box from the floor with shaking fingers. It played a soft melody when he popped it open, and he stared at the crushed velvet lining the bottom.

"Dad."

"Your mama's weddin' ring was in here." He swallowed hard and closed the lid before setting the box back on the mantel where it had been this morning.

Marx hadn't even noticed that she wasn't wearing it. "Why?"

"Didn't fit no more." Sweat beaded across his forehead and upper lip, and he swiped it away with his fingers before letting out a tight breath.

Concerned, Marx suggested, "Why don't you sit down."

Dad swatted aside the hand Marx extended toward him. "I'm fine. I don't need to be coddled like some . . ." he trailed off, struggling to catch his breath.

Marx caught his arm and led him to the recliner, lowering him into it with more gentleness than he ever thought he would handle his father with. "Is it your heart?"

Dad pressed a hand to his chest. "I don't . . . know."

"Stay put. I'm gonna find some aspirin." He walked back to the front door to call in the girls. He hadn't had time to secure the rest of the house, but if someone was still on the property, the girls would be safer inside with him than outside alone.

He went to the kitchen to grab the bottle of aspirin from the medicine cabinet, but the cabinet was empty. In their search for anything worth stealing, the thief had rifled through the cupboards and left the contents scattered across the counter and floor.

Marx crouched to search through the boxes and cans of food for the aspirin. Where was it? It had to be there. Growing desperate, he began throwing things across the kitchen to get them out of his way.

He couldn't find it. "Mama, where do you keep the aspirin?"

"In the kitchen," she called back. "But we don't need it."

Marx returned to the living room to find Dad folded over in the recliner, his face buried in his hands as his shoulders shook silently. Mama rubbed his back and cast Marx a look of grief that made his chest ache.

"It ain't his heart. He's just upset."

Tears shimmered in her eyes, and a fresh wave of anger toward the intruder crashed over Marx. Someone was going to regret making his mama cry.

"I promised . . . it would never . . . happen again," Dad said between heavy breaths.

The guilt and sense of failure his dad was feeling right now was something Marx was intimately familiar with. His gaze traveled to Holly, who was crouched near the tree, sorting through the broken ornaments.

He had promised her that her foster brother would never touch her again, and then he had failed to protect her. She didn't blame him, but he felt responsible just the same.

A tap drew Marx's attention to the front door. Darian stood on the porch, a grim expression on his face. He gestured him inside, and Darian stepped carefully through the evidence in his sneakers.

"Sneakers?"

Darian unzipped his winter jacket to reveal a Georgia Bulldogs sweatshirt. "It's my day off."

"Sorry you gotta work."

"It's part of the job. You know how it goes."

He did. When he was working a case, he seldom had days off or full nights of sleep. But many of his cases were homicides rather than nuisance calls and home invasions. "Mama. Darian's here."

She patted his father's arm before coming to speak with them. She lowered her voice. "He's havin' a hard time with this. So I'll tell you what I can."

"Do you know what was taken?" Darian asked.

"Oh goodness." Mama exhaled. "I haven't had a chance to check."

"They took Dad's guns, Mama's weddin' ring, and the TV." Marx nodded toward the empty TV stand.

Mama's hand went to her heart and she looked at the box on the mantel with fresh tears flowing down her cheeks. "My ring? But I was savin' that for,"—her eyes shifted to Holly and then away— "for when I had a grandbaby to pass it on to."

Marx rubbed her arm. "We'll get it back, Mama."

Darian pulled a small notebook and pen from his hoodie pocket. "How much is the ring worth?"

Mama wiped the dampness from her face. "1,500 dollars, maybe. I don't really remember too well."

"You got a picture?"

"Not offhand, but I can sort through our pictures later. If it helps, it had our names engraved on the inside, though I imagine they can erase that these days."

Darian turned to Marx. "You mentioned guns. What kind and how many should I be lookin' for?"

"I don't know. It's been a long time since I've seen them all." Marx folded his arms. "You think this might have somethin' to do with the person Holly saw outside the window?"

"He could've been casin' the place. With the robberies we've had lately, I wouldn't be surprised."

Whoever had broken in had probably been disappointed. His family was neither affluent nor materialistic, and there was very little worth stealing.

"I'll call in CSU. Maybe they can find some fingerprints or fibers that'll lead us to the perpetrator." Darian pulled out his phone and walked back outside to place the call.

Marx touched Mama's shoulder to let her know he would be right back and walked over to Holly, who was staring at the ceramic angel ornament in her hands with a pinched expression.

"This one's a little chipped," she said when he approached. "But I think we can fix it with some glue."

She would spend the rest of the night hunting down pieces and gluing ornaments back together if it would ease his mama's sadness.

"I'm sure we can, but I doubt that one-winged angel is the reason for your expression."

Gingerly, she placed the remains of the angel on the mantel above the fireplace. "I can't remember his face. The guy outside the window. He's just . . . a blur."

"That's not your fault. It was dark, you were tired, and it was a split-second glimpse. Nobody expects you to draw a portrait."

"But if he's the person who broke in, I can't even help Detective Darian with a description. Tall, young-ish guy doesn't really give him much to work with." She sighed and looked down at the bracelet on her wrist—

161

one of two pieces of jewelry she treasured. "That ring means a lot to your mom. How do we get it back for her?"

"We let Darian do his job."

"He's not you."

Marx smiled. "Meanin', you don't *trust* him to do his job." She responded to his statement with a noncommittal shrug of one shoulder. "I remember when you didn't trust me, either."

She scrunched up her face in feigned confusion. "I don't know what you're talking about."

He laughed. "You're a terrible liar. And there *are* other detectives who do their job well. I'm not one of a kind."

She offered him one of her heart melting smiles and wiggled her way under his arm to give him a hug. "Yes, you are."

His lips twitched as he held back a smile. "Are you tryin' to win this disagreement with cuteness?"

"Is it working?"

"Yes." He kissed her on the forehead. "And don't worry about my mama's ring. If Darian doesn't find it, I will." He left her to continue picking through the disaster on the floor and joined Darian in the hall. "Well?"

"CSU will be here . . ."—he leaned to see past Marx, his attention snagging on Holly— "shortly. What is she doin'?" He didn't wait for an answer before calling out, "Hey, uh, sweetheart, you mind leavin' things where they are until CSU gets their photos?"

Holly glared at him and proceeded to pick up the ornament she found. Darian looked at Marx for help.

"Don't call her sweetheart," Marx said before addressing Holly. "Sweetheart, why don't you leave things for now. We'll work on it later."

Darian frowned in confusion. "But you just said—"

"*You* can't call her sweetheart. I never said I can't. She—"

Screaming, base-pounding rock music erupted from the neighbor's house, so loud that it pulsed through the floor beneath Marx's feet. "Aren't they breakin' some kind of noise ordinance?"

Darian glanced at his watch. "Between ten at night and ten in the mornin'. Right now they're just bein' obnoxious. Is this a normal thing for them?"

"Seems to be. Can't you do somethin'?"

"Considerin' it's unlawful to cause excessive noise that unreasonably interferes with the comfort of residents within the city's jurisdiction, I can."

"Did you memorize the entire law book?"

"I'm single. What do you think?"

Before either of them could head for the door, Marx's dad pushed past them and stormed out of the house.

24

Now

Gus knew who was responsible for the break in; it was that irritating kid, Alex, and now he was throwing one of his juvenile parties as if he hadn't a care in the world.

Well Gus was going to give him something to care about. He tightened his grip on his shovel as he stomped toward the booming noise that kids these days called music.

Alex and four other kids sat on hunks of wood around a bonfire, setting marshmallows on fire and throwing back beers. Gus fixed his sites on the speaker system sitting on the bed of a truck.

He swung and knocked the first speaker to the ground, pounding it with the shovel and punting it across the yard. He went after the second one, determined to smash them both to bits.

A hand gripped his arm, and he swung the shovel on reflex, narrowly missing the punk's head.

"I know it was you!" Gus shouted, brandishing the shovel at the stunned group of kids. "I know you broke into my house!"

"Ain't nobody broke into your house, old man!" Alex fired back. "You ain't got nothin' worth stealin'!"

Gus knocked the second speaker to the ground and speared it with the tip of the shovel, cutting out the last of the music. "Where's my wife's ring?!"

Alex lunged for him, but Richard stepped in the way, shoving him back a step. "You don't touch my family."

"Your pops here busted up my speakers. Who's gonna pay for that?"

"If those are your speakers, then you're the one I'm gonna arrest for breakin' the noise ordinance," Darian explained. "Are you sure they're your speakers?"

Alex sputtered soundlessly, then threw up his arms. "Fine. Forget the speakers."

"Probably a good idea. Hey! I didn't say you could leave!" Darian went after the kids trying to scatter. "Come here!"

Alex pointed a finger at Gus. "Get your wrinkled bag of bones off my grass. And you—" he shifted his finger to Richard—"if you can't keep a leash on your daddy, put him in a home where he belongs."

Heat rushed up Gus's neck into his face, and he surged forward, raising the shovel to swing at the punk's head. "I've had enough of you and your disrespect!"

Richard wrenched the shovel from his grip before he could knock the kid's block off. "Knock it off."

"What do you think I was tryin' to do?!" Gus roared, his breath becoming harder to keep a hold of. He reached for his shovel. "Give it back."

Richard flung it a good twenty or thirty feet in the other direction. "You want your shovel, go home and get it. And stay there."

"This . . . good for nothin' lowlife broke into my home! Stole my guns and your mama's ring." Something in his chest tightened as his anger climbed. "And you're just gonna stand there?"

"You need to calm down, Dad."

"Rick! Snag that one!" Darian hollered.

A kid, no more than fifteen, tried to skirt past them in his haste to escape. Richard caught a fistful of his shirt and flung him to the ground. Gus took advantage of his son's distraction and walked up to Alex.

"The cops might not be able to prove what you did, but I don't need proof."

"Get out of my face, old man."

Alex shoved him back a step and Gus stumbled over a rock in the yard, losing his balance. Pain exploded in his right hip when he hit the ground, shooting down his leg and up his back like a bolt of lightning, setting fire to every nerve in its path.

He struggled to catch his breath in between the urge to vomit and the urge to pass out. As he tried to breathe, the sharpness in his chest returned—that too-familiar feeling of a fist closing around his heart and lungs, squeezing until his insides felt like they were being crushed.

Not again, Lord.

He clawed at his chest, trying in vain to loosen the grip around his heart. His vision blurred, but he heard his son's voice as gentle hands lowered him to his back on the ground. And then Martha was there, holding his hand, and Holly spoke to him as she covered him with a blanket.

He realized he was probably going to die tonight. But at least he got to tell Richard the truth—that he never wanted to hurt him, and that he was sorry.

25

Now

Holly watched anxiously as Mr. Gus was loaded into the ambulance. She prayed that he would be all right.

Please, please, please, Jesus.

Even though Marx and his father didn't seem to get along, Marx loved him. It was obvious by the worry in his eyes as the paramedics tended to his dad.

Ms. Martha ignored the protest of the paramedics and climbed into the back of the ambulance to ride to the hospital with her husband.

"The doors ain't gonna shut themselves," she said impatiently, and the uniformed man closed one door with a roll of his eyes, climbed in, and pulled the other door shut.

Holly's gaze drifted to the officers who were loading the kids from the neighbor's house into the back of squad cars. "So, you guys can search Alex's house for the stolen stuff now, right? Because he committed a crime?"

"Unfortunately, no. It doesn't work that way," Marx said. "For us to search his house for stolen property, we need somethin' more than a hunch to take to a judge. No judge is gonna issue a warrant without probable cause."

Frustrated, she folded her arms and glared at the neighboring house. Her gut told her Alex and those kids were involved.

"Yeah, I understand my rights, but I ain't done nothin'," Alex protested from a few feet away.

Detective Darian checked to make sure the handcuffs were secure. "If you think shovin' somebody to the ground is nothin', then you have a very lousy understandin' of the law."

"I didn't push him to the ground. He tripped."

Darian gripped his upper arm and tugged him away toward his car. Holly bent to pick up the blanket she had used to cover Mr. Gus. "Do you think Alex and those kids were behind the break-in?"

"Very likely." Marx watched the ambulance and squad cars bump and rock down the drive onto the street. "Go grab your coat and we'll head to the hospital."

Holly glanced at the house and then back at him. "I'm gonna stay here."

He turned a disapproving frown on her. "Not by yourself, you're not."

"Yes, by myself. The neighbor and kids were arrested, so it's not like they can break in again. Besides,

I don't want your parents to come back to their home in pieces. I wanna clean it up."

"You don't have to do that, Holly."

"I want to. I'll lock the doors and I promise I'll keep my phone on me at all times."

"I'm not sure it's a good idea."

She understood his reluctance, but he couldn't watch over her all the time. She needed to recover the sense of independence that fear had stripped away and regain her self-confidence.

"I'm staying."

He blew out a breath as he looked up at the night sky.

He reminded her so much of her dad in this moment, the way he had struggled with her show of independence when she was eight years old. She had *informed* her dad that she would be walking to school from the family bookstore on her own. He hadn't taken the news well, but he eventually allowed her to spread her wings. Before long, she was walking her sister and her best friend to school.

"All right," Marx conceded. "But you call me if anythin' makes you feel uneasy."

She hugged him tightly. "Okay." He would leave the hospital to come pick her up if she got scared or uncomfortable, which was why she didn't intend for either of those things to happen.

She released him and headed up the steps into the house, giving him a finger-wave goodbye before closing the door.

"I'm not leavin' 'til I hear that door lock," he called out, and she snapped the deadbolt.

She listened for the retreating sound of his car before turning to face the silent, empty house. She nearly jumped out of her shoes when the old house let out an ogre-deep groan.

"Just old wood," she told herself, pushing away from the door to get to work.

If there was one thing she was good at, it was cleaning. She could spend an entire day in Cinderella's sooty slippers just to escape from the stresses of life.

The kitchen would be a good place to start.

She tracked down a broom, trash bags, and rubber gloves in a cleaning closet and, armed for battle, tackled the chaos. She salvaged what she could and bagged what she couldn't.

She sucked on homemade cherry candies as she worked. It was strange—she had only been eating Ms. Martha's cooking for a few days, but her jeans were starting to feel a little snug. Maybe her friend Jace had a point when she told Holly to stop buying jeans and start buying more leggings. But she liked jeans.

She could stop eating candy. She stared at the tasty cherry treat resting on her palm, conflicted, then shrugged and popped it into her mouth. She would just buy bigger jeans.

By the time she finished with the kitchen, it was nearly perfect. She worked her way down the hall and into the living room, singing Christmas songs as she went.

Ms. Martha had probably collected ornaments over the years the way Holly's mother had—some representing cherished memories and milestones—and it was heartbreaking to see them scattered throughout the room in irreparable pieces.

She picked up part of a clay ornament with a child's handprint stamped on it. The other half was in three smaller chunks, and when she pushed them together, she noticed the initials at the bottom: CAM.

Marx had mentioned a sister with a strange C-name once. Charisma? Chastity? She couldn't remember. But it did get her wondering about Marx's initials again. RDM.

Demitri? Delorean? The third name that popped into her head was girly enough that most men would be embarrassed to share it. She snickered as she fished her phone from her pocket and sent the name to Marx with a question mark.

Daphne?

She wasn't sure he would know what she was talking about, but his response removed all doubt.

Really? You honestly think my mama named me Richard Daphne Marx?

Funny how he avoided confirming or denying it. But that couldn't be it. She would figure it out eventually.

She sent him a quick text, asking about his parents, but seconds ticked by without an answer, making her anxious.

Mr. Gus was going to be okay, wasn't he? People survived heart attacks all the time. But he'd been so pale lying in the grass . . .

She squeezed her eyes shut and whispered a prayer. Marx and his dad were so close to working things out, and it couldn't end this way. He let out a breath when her phone chirped with an incoming text message.

Marx had finally answered.

They're running more tests, but he's stable for the moment. Mama's a little stressed, but otherwise fine. Everything okay there?

She assured him that all was well, then shoved her phone back into her pocket. She caught sight of the jewelry box on the mantel and opened it, a soft tune filling the air. The box was empty. Was this where Ms. Martha kept her ring?

Her attention drifted to the window, and she eyed the dark house next door. The police had taken Alex and the boys in for questioning, which meant the house should be empty for at least another few hours.

26

Now

Holly stood on tiptoes outside of the neighbor's house to see through the unlit window. She wiped away a patch of grunge on the glass with the sleeve of her shirt and peered inside.

The police needed a warrant to go into the house to collect evidence, but they needed evidence to get a warrant. None of it made any sense to her, especially when everyone suspected Alex was guilty.

She glanced at the trashcan beside her. She *could* climb on top of it and wriggle through the small window, but she was pretty sure she would end up flat on her back in the grass, smothered in trash.

Nope, checking the door first.

She climbed the steps to the back door and wiggled the handle. It turned. It boggled her mind that so many people left their homes unlocked and vulnerable.

She bit her bottom lip as she stood at the threshold, unsure what to do next. Technically, going inside wasn't breaking and entering, right? She hadn't broken anything.

She glanced down at the worn and mud-caked doormat beneath her boots that declared in curly letters, *Come on in.*

"Okay."

She stepped inside the empty house and immediately staggered back, pressing the back of her wrist against her nose when the unmistakable stench of body odor and rotten food slammed into her. The smell tap danced on her gag reflex, threatening to make her retch.

She was pretty sure if she stuck her head in the trash can outside, it would smell better.

Reaching into her hoodie pouch, she fished out one of the green spearmint candies and popped it into her mouth. That would help take the edge off.

"Why didn't I bring a flashlight?"

And some mace, and a knife, and some hand sanitizer.

She tried not to imagine what she was touching as she slid her hand along the wall, feeling for a light switch. She was going to take a long, hot shower when she got back.

With lots and lots of soap.

She brushed a smooth plastic surface on the wall with her fingertips and found a switch. She flipped it up, expecting light to flood the kitchen, but something growled to life beside her.

175

She yelped and stumbled sideways, her heart slamming against her ribs. Whatever it was clanged and thumped out of sync like an elementary school band, and it took her a second to realize it was a garbage disposal. She may have accidentally dropped a metal measuring spoon or two into Marx's disposal before, and it sounded about the same. She slapped the switch back down and the grinding and clanging quieted.

"This is such a bad idea."

But the tears and grief shining in Ms. Martha's eyes as she spoke about her ring lingered in Holly's mind. Marx's mother was a sweet person, and she didn't deserve any of the awful things that had happened to her family tonight.

There was nothing Holly could do to help with Mr. Gus's heart attack or to help Ms. Martha feel secure in her home after it had been invaded and ripped apart. But maybe she could find the ring.

The man who designed this house had apparently been drunk at the time, because he put the switch for the living room ceiling fan next to the garbage disposal switch, and the one for the light in the living room.

"Ew," she said with a scrunch of her nose. The house looked as filthy as it smelled.

She uncapped her camera lens and lifted the camera. She took snapshots of the house as she crept through it, the trash on the floor crunching beneath her feet like dry leaves.

The photographer in her started mentally nitpicking the angles and lighting, and she had to remind herself that this wasn't a photoshoot. This was . . . work. Her first adventure into crime scene photography.

She captured the game systems, high-end electronics—including any information stickers on them that might help the police identify where they came from—and the giant flat screen TV. If she turned it sideways, it might almost be as tall as her.

Apparently, Alex was familiar with every game system on the market, but a broom and dust pan were beyond him.

She snapped a picture of a really nice bike in the corner. She wouldn't mind a bike. But not that one. It was bumblebee yellow. Ick.

She made her way into the bedroom, opening dresser drawers, which were either empty or stuffed with wadded up clothes. Marx, who liked everything perfectly neat and organized, wouldn't know what to do with this place. He would probably have nightmares about pants being mixed in with the T-shirts.

A soft laugh bubbled out of her. She should do that when they got back to New York. Oh, the havoc she could wreak on his dresser and closet while he was at work.

She checked under the bed and in the nightstand before zeroing in on the closet. There was a hanging rack, but all of the clothes were tossed on the floor. She nudged them aside with her boot. Nothing.

Dragging a chair over from the room across the hall, she climbed up to see what Alex was hiding on the top shelf in the closet. She rolled her eyes in disgust at the pile of sleazy magazines and bypassed them for a small metal box in the corner.

She opened it and sighed, disappointed to find his heroin stash rather than jewelry. This guy needed some serious help before he ended up dead on his kitchen floor with a needle in his arm. She took pictures before closing the box.

Where would he hide the jewelry?

She hadn't checked the bathroom or the kitchen cupboards. She hopped down from the chair and started back down the hall when a door closed.

She stopped in her tracks.

The boys were all supposed to be at the police station. Had they let them go already?

"Who's there?" a man called out, and Holly's heart jumped into her throat. It wasn't Alex, and his voice was far too mature to belong to a teenager.

She needed to hide. She opened the door closest to her and terror wrapped around her insides. It was a long, narrow staircase into a pitch-black basement.

Cement floors and stone walls, darkness . . . the air around her began to thin, and no matter how much she gasped, she couldn't get enough oxygen. She couldn't go down there. No one knew she was here. What if he locked her in?

What if he hurt her?

Breathe, she told herself. Marx would never let that happen. He would look for her here, even if he had to break down the door to do it.

The sound of the man kicking things out of his path as he headed her way jarred her into motion. "Disgustin' mess."

She placed her feet on the top step, refusing to go down any further, and pulled the door close to the frame, gripping the knob so tightly that her fingers ached.

She could feel the panic attack closing in around her, suffocating her and threatening to send her spiraling back into that nightmare.

I'm not there, I'm not there, I'm not there, she chanted silently, trying to wrench herself from the memory's tightening grip.

The man came down the hall, pausing near the basement door, so close that she could see three red dots tattooed beneath his left eye.

Was it a gang symbol? Some kind of prison tattoo? She tried to stop her mind from racing through the frightening possibilities. Maybe he just liked dots.

"Who's in here?"

Holly trembled so badly that her left foot nearly slipped down another step, and she had to clutch the railing for balance. The carpeted step beneath her let out the faintest groan, and she held her breath, praying he hadn't heard it.

The knob was suddenly yanked from her grip, and a man nearly as wide as he was tall, filled the opening. He stared at her with an unreadable expression, and nausea rolled through her.

Was he going to try to hurt her? How could she get out? There was no way around him.

He swiped a meaty hand out and she stumbled down a few more steps. The man said something to her as light ignited the stairwell, but all she could hear was her heart thundering in her ears as he thumped down the steps, driving her closer to that terrifying prison.

27

Now

Marx paced in front of the vending machines at the hospital, his concern growing as his third call to Holly's cell rolled over to voicemail. She had promised to keep her phone on her.

"If you don't call me back in the next five minutes, I'm comin' home." He snapped his phone shut with a frustrated sigh.

Holly was a magnet for trouble.

Whether she was minding her own business or sticking her little nose where it didn't belong, trouble found her. It was the times when she went looking for it that concerned him the most. Usually, she thought she was being helpful.

She was up to something. He was almost certain of it. He glanced at his phone and resisted the urge to call her again. If she was able or willing to answer her phone, she would call him back.

He stuffed his cell in his pocket, filled two paper cups of coffee from the machine, and carried them back to the hospital room.

"Any answer from Holly?" Mama asked the moment he stepped through the curtain.

He hadn't mentioned that he was going to call her, but she knew him too well. "I tried to reach her three times."

She accepted the coffee. "She'll be all right."

Dad drew in a breath and let out a moan of longing. "Is that regular coffee?"

"Not for you." Marx dropped into the guest chair beside Mama and checked his watch.

Dad let out a grunt of dissatisfaction. "With my luck, those idiots who broke in stole everythin' worthwhile and left the decaf coffee."

"If you'd rather have no coffee, I can make that happen," Mama informed him before taking a drink from her cup.

Dad crossed his arms over his blanket and huffed. "Why you gotta be so sour?"

"Quit your gripin'. Ain't nobody wants to hear it. Besides, you're gonna raise your blood pressure some more and the doctor's gonna have a cow."

"You should listen to your wife." The voice preceded an older woman by less than a second, and she brushed aside the curtain to enter the room. "She's a smart lady." She smiled and offered a nod of greeting to everyone in the room. "Hello. I'm Doctor Bashar, a member of the cardiovascular team at the hospital."

"Good," Marx's dad said. "Tell them I'm fine and I can go home."

She walked to the foot of the hospital bed, angling her body so that everyone could see her. "I understand your eagerness to go home, Mr. Marx, but this is your third heart attack in two years. I would prefer to keep you overnight for observation."

"I don't need to be observed. I'm goin' home."

"That's of course your decision, but it is against my medical advice. I also understand you've made significant lifestyle changes since your last heart attack. Unfortunately, it is not enough."

"What do you mean, it ain't enough? I haven't had a cookie, butter, or regular coffee since God said 'let there be light.' What else am I supposed to do?"

She smiled understandingly. "It is vital that you keep your stress level down. Yoga has been shown to—"

"Yoga? Somebody just broke into our house, and you expect me to stand on my head, singin' Kum ba yah?"

"I apologize. I was not aware."

"What do we need to do?" Mama asked, redirecting the conversation.

"Continue with the dietary changes. Add mild exercise—nothing strenuous. And try to reduce stress."

"If he's stressin' himself out, does that mean I can knock him unconscious?" Marx asked, and Doctor Bashar smiled.

"I would not recommend it. In that instance, perhaps some warm chamomile tea would be best. I'll send the nurse in with the discharge papers. And I do want to say, Mr. Marx, that you were very lucky tonight. You may not be so lucky next time. Please take your medications and do as we discussed."

"Thank you, Doctor," Mama said as Doctor Bashar made her way toward the exit. "And Merry Christmas."

Doctor Bashar paused. "I'm Hindu, but I appreciate the sentiment. I wish you all a very peaceful, spiritual holiday."

28

Now

Holly opened her eyes and blinked up at a cobwebbed ceiling. She was lying on something soft and lumpy, and she tried to rearrange her foggy memories into an order that made sense.

She'd been cleaning the house when she decided to snoop around next door. She'd been on her way back to the kitchen and then a door had closed. The man, the basement.

She scrambled up so quickly that she fell over the side of the couch and landed on the floor, shredded candy wrappers surrounding her like a bed of leaves.

"Oh good, you're not dead."

The man's voice sent a fresh jolt of fear through her, and she groped along the floor for a weapon, wrapping her fingers around a fork.

He sat on the edge of a folding chair with a bored and tired expression on his face. "You passed out in the basement. I caught you before you hit the floor. Carried you up here. Good thing you don't weigh much more than a hundred pound sack of flour."

She climbed to her feet, keeping a solid grip on the fork. As self-defense weapons went, it was pretty lousy, but it was better than a spoon.

"I work in a bakery," he clarified, and she noticed the patches of white on his clothes. "My nephew was supposed to help me unpack the flour shipment tonight. He didn't show. Thought maybe he'd be here."

He rose to his full, intimidating height, and Holly stepped back, putting more space between them. She knew that if he'd wanted to, he could've hurt her while they were downstairs or while she was unconscious, but she still didn't trust him.

The man glanced dismissively at the fork she held as he pulled a jacket off the back of the chair and shrugged it on over his wide shoulders. "Took me a bit to put your face to the story, but I recognize you. You're that girl everybody was lookin' for this past spring. Snatched by some pervert."

Holly's stomach turned over. Even clear across the country, she couldn't escape her past.

"That bein' what it is, I ain't gonna take it personal that you're pointin' a fork at me." He zipped up his coat and adjusted the bunched collar. "I just wanted to make sure you was all right before I left."

She tried to swallow the guilt that lodged in her throat and lowered the fork to her side. "Thanks."

A hint of a smile lifted the left corner of his mouth. "Don't talk much, do ya?"

She wasn't sure how to answer that, so she decided to say nothing. Belatedly, she realized that her silence only confirmed his suspicion.

"My nephew mentioned there was a girl moved in with the old couple next door. Described you right down to them there purple boots." He jutted his chin toward her feet. "For somebody sneakin' into other people's houses, you certainly don't dress the part."

She looked down at her rain boots. She hadn't really thought about that; maybe she should've worn sneakers. But these were her favorite.

She wiggled her toes, enjoying the spaciousness of her rain boots. "I like these boots. And you snuck in, too."

"Lookin' for my nephew. Not lookin' for whatever you're here lookin' for. You seen him around?"

She studied the man—he had dark hair and eyes with Latino highlights, but she didn't remember anyone who looked like him. "I don't know."

The man folded his arms, the movement making him appear even bigger, and she tried not to fidget. "I make you nervous."

She shrugged a shoulder.

"I make most people nervous. I'm a big man." He sat back down in the chair and the joints squeaked in protest. "Tends to happen when you eat most of what you bake. I'm George, by the way."

"Holly. I like baking, but I'm not very good at it."

He smiled and it softened the features that had seemed so harsh a moment before. "As much as I'd love to fix your recipes, I'm tired. So if you know anythin' about my nephew . . ."

"There are a lot of boys that hang out here. I don't know any of their names though."

George sighed and rubbed at the creases in his forehead where streaks of white flour had settled. "Yeah, I'm tryin' to keep Bryce away from Martin. He ain't a bad kid, but Martin . . . he ain't got a lick of sense, and I wouldn't trust him to clean my toilet, let alone be an example to my sister's boy."

Holly swallowed. Should she tell him that his nephew might have been arrested? "There was a break in next door—"

"They're happenin' all over the neighborhood. Cops ain't doin' nothin' about it. Say they ain't got any suspects."

"They do now."

George pinned her with a hard look. "Bryce ain't no thief, if that's where you're headin'. He's a good kid. And he gets paid for workin' at the bakery. He don't need to steal."

"I don't know if he was involved or not, but the police came earlier and noticed the boys were drinking and—"

George swore. "He went and got himself arrested?"

"If he was with them, then yeah."

"I didn't think this day could get worse." As he pushed himself out of the chair, it leaned to the left, on the verge of collapsing.

"George," Holly said, catching his attention before he could walk out the door. "I hope everything works out for your family. And thanks for, um, catching me before I hit the floor."

He made a sucking sound with the corner of his mouth as he looked at her. "I'm gonna give you some friendly advice. Sneakin' into houses is liable to get you into trouble, and I don't just mean with the law. Girl like you sneaks into the wrong house . . . well . . . you know what happens."

She wrapped her arms around herself and nodded. "I know. Thanks for the advice."

She was about to follow him out when she remembered the reason she had come. The ring. She still hadn't found it. But where . . .

Her eyes swept over the house one last time before drifting back to the sink. Hmm. She walked over to the broken garbage disposal and peered down into the grimy hole.

It would be a good place to hide something, especially since no one would want to stick their hand down there. She scanned the floor for a plastic bag and found one from the local department store. She wrapped it around her hand and secured it with a hairband before diving in.

She felt around until she hit something solid. She pulled out a small, metal tin with Looney Tunes characters on it and popped the lid off. She found a folded Ziploc bag filled with expensive-looking jewelry.

She catalogued the cluster of items with three quick photos, then opened the Ziploc bag and carefully fingered through the contents. The third diamond ring she examined had an inscription on the inside band: *Martha & Gus.*

28

Now

Mama rifled through her purse, searching for her keys to the front door. "You worry about that girl too much."

If she knew how much trouble Holly could get into while standing still, she would be worried, too. Marx glanced at his phone one last time to be certain he hadn't missed a call from her.

"Oh, for heaven's sakes." Mama overturned her purse and dumped the contents onto the chair beside the door.

It would never cease to amaze Marx how much miscellaneous junk a woman could squeeze into her purse. And they wondered why they could never find anything.

The keys were the last to tumble out, and Mama snatched them up before shoving everything else back into her bag. "I swear, I'd lose my head if it wasn't attached." She unlocked the door and gasped. "Oh my goodness."

"What's the matter now?" Dad asked as Marx helped him up the steps onto the porch. His hip wasn't broken, but it was bruised badly enough that he would be limping for a few days.

Mama walked into the clean hallway, her mouth hanging open in astonishment. She made her way down the hall to the living room and paused in the doorway, her hand going to her heart. "Oh, Ritchie. Come look."

Marx left his dad leaning against the door frame and walked quickly to Mama's side. The living room had been tidied up, the tree straightened, and recently patched ornaments were propped on the mantel above the fireplace.

Half of a wooden snowman rested in Holly's palm, a fingers-twitch away from tumbling to the floor. Holly lay slumped over on the couch pillows, an open bottle of glue hugged to her chest and a half-eaten cookie on a plate in front of the couch.

Marx sighed, relieved that she was all right.

Mama walked to the couch and removed the glue and snowman from Holly's slack fingers, then draped a blanket over her. The warmth in her eyes as she brushed a strand of hair back from Holly's face was one of love.

Straightening, she whispered, "I'm gonna keep her."

Marx smiled. Holly had a way of finding a place in people's hearts without even trying, and Marx had known his mama was doomed the moment the two met.

"She's twenty-eight years old, Mama. You can't just keep her."

"Sure as I'm a God-fearin' woman I can. This baby needs a family, and just so happens I got plenty of love to give. Besides, even your daddy's warmin' up to her."

Marx looked back at his dad, who cleared his throat at the sappy exchange of words. "She's likable enough, I s'pose."

Holly let out a moan and shifted on the cushions. Marx pressed a finger to his lips and motioned his parents from the room. He didn't want them to wake her.

Mama's jewelry box sat at the other end of the couch near Holly's feet. Why had Holly taken it off the mantel? When he picked it up to put it back where it belonged, something shifted. He opened the lid and stared in stunned disbelief at the ring resting on the crushed velvet bottom.

He was so captivated by the presence of the ring that Holly's voice startled him.

"I found it."

He looked down at her as he closed the box, cutting off the quiet melody that had probably woken her. "Where?"

She scooted into a seated position on the couch, her demeanor cautious. "Please don't be mad."

"Why don't you tell me where you found it and then I'll decide whether or not I'm mad." When she flicked a furtive glance toward the window, his tone took on an edge of impatience. "Holly."

"I sort of . . . stole it back."

"Meanin', you broke into Alex Martin's house."

"I didn't break anything. And the door was unlocked."

"It doesn't matter, Holly!" She cringed, reminding him that he needed to watch his temper. More calmly, he explained, "What you did is illegal. You could go to jail. Do you understand that?"

"I'm sorry. I was just trying to help."

He rubbed the back of his neck as he tried to figure out what to do next. "Is there any proof you were in his house?"

She nodded toward her camera on the metal dinner tray. "I took some pictures."

Marx grabbed her camera and scrolled through the digital images. For a man who worked a blue collar job, Alex Martin had an excessive number of electronics. Pairing that with the heroin in his closet, he had to be supplementing his income somehow.

"He's stealing things," Holly said. "And not just from your parents. There were thousands of dollars of jewelry in that tin he keeps stuffed in the drain."

Marx turned off the camera and set it aside. What was he supposed to do now? If he told her to delete the pictures and say nothing, he would be betraying his duty to the law. And how many other people would Alex Martin victimize? But if he handed the pictures over, Holly could go to jail.

"Okay. I'm gonna talk to Darian first thing in the mornin'. See if there's a way to handle this without you gettin' in trouble."

"What if he arrests me?"

He crouched and cupped her face in his hands, trying to reassure her. "I'm not gonna let that happen. All right? I need you to trust me."

She nodded.

"Okay." He kissed her forehead before rising. "Now go get some sleep."

He waited for to head upstairs before going into the kitchen to explain the situation to his parents. He needed to make sure that Holly was protected, no matter how things turned out tomorrow morning. "If things with Darian don't go as planned—"

"Don't you worry," Mama broke in. "I'll drive her across state lines myself if I got to. I ain't about to let nobody arrest that sweet baby."

Marx smiled and hugged her, grateful that he could rely on her to watch over Holly in his absence.

30

Now

Darian blew out a breath as he sat on the edge of his desk, clicking through the pictures on Holly's camera. "If I could, I would hire her on as my personal crime scene photographer. Girl's thorough, and she's got an excellent eye for angles and lightin'."

Marx crossed his arms. "I'm not really concerned about her career as a photographer at the moment."

"Right." Darian placed the camera gently on his desk. "She did break the law."

"The door was unlocked, and she didn't damage anythin'. She was just tryin' to help."

"I understand that, Rick, I do. But as a cop, you know it's not our job to pick and choose who does the time and who skates on the crime. That's up to the D.A."

"She's been through enough."

Darian folded his arms and sighed. "I know. I did some research after I met her, and I have no desire to traumatize that girl any further by lockin' her in a cell. But you gotta understand the position this puts me in."

"There's gotta be a way around it."

"It all depends on whether or not Alex Martin wants to press charges. And considerin' Holly had him arrested for battery, I think he's gonna jump at the chance to get back at her."

Marx scrubbed his hands over his face, the stress eating away at his nerves. "The pictures are at least proof that Alex Martin is a thief."

"Except for the fact that they were illegally obtained, sure. The problem is, the moment a judge learns that they were taken by somebody who broke into Martin's house, he's gonna kick us out of the courtroom for wastin' his time." Darian tapped his fingers on his biceps, thinking. "I might have an idea."

Alex Martin sat in the interrogation room, his dark hair matted to his forehead, and his handcuffs rattling on the table as he vibrated in his chair.

Marx watched from the opposite side of the one-way mirror as Darian stepped into the room, tossing a folder onto the table hard enough to send pictures sliding out, and dropped into the opposite chair.

"What's this?" Alex pulled one of the pictures closer, the patch of dry skin between his eyebrows crinkling and flaking. "Wha . . ." He dragged the others over and spread them out across the table.

"As you can see, we have visual confirmation that you're harborin' stolen property in your house," Darian explained.

Alex slapped the table. "You can't go in my house without a warrant!"

"I didn't go anywhere near your house. In fact, no cops went anywhere near your house." Darian leaned forward and tapped the stack of pictures with a finger. "These were takin' by a concerned young lady."

"Who?"

"*Who* isn't the point. The point is, we got you."

"You got nothin'. And I want a name."

Darian leaned back in his chair. "I ain't givin' you the name of the photographer."

Alex sorted through the photos again and pulled one from the pile, one that had captured just the tip of Holly's purple rain boot next to the game systems. His face reddened with rage. "Her?!" He flung the pictures off the table. "That crazy chick with the eggs broke into my house? I want her arrested."

"I'm not here to talk about her. And if you're smart, you'll let it go and concentrate on the fact that you're in a lot of trouble."

Alex leaned across the table and shoved a finger in Darian's face. "She thinks she can have me jammed up for no good reason and then bust into my house? I ain't lettin' her get away with that."

Marx's arms tightened over his chest as he watched the interrogation through the one-way mirror. It wasn't so much Alex's choice of words that bothered him; it was the threat in his tone when he spoke them.

Darian laughed, but it deteriorated into a choking cough when Alex glared at him. "You're serious."

"Yeah, I'm serious."

"You realize girls like her get away with everythin'. It's been happenin' since the dawn of time. She's petite, she's gorgeous, and I bet if she cries, every man in the room is gonna trip over himself to hand her a tissue."

Marx smiled. That last bit was probably true.

Darian pulled out his pen and notebook. "Let's talk about the jewelry. I already know about Mrs. Marx's ring. Where'd you get the rest of it?"

"I got no use for jewelry. Maybe that girl planted it so you'd drag me in here." His anger slowly gave way to cocky amusement. "Yeah, she broke into my house to take those pictures, which means they ain't legal. You got squat, little piggy."

Darian tapped the end of his pen against the notepad. "Nah, she already had you arrested for puttin' your disgustin' hands on her. Had you locked up like some pathetic pervert. If she wanted to humiliate you, I think she got the point across the first time, don't you?"

Alex's fingers clenched into fists and his lips pressed together so tightly that they drained of color. "I want you to arrest her. Drag *her* down here in handcuffs.

And while y'all are trippin' over yourselves to hand her tissues when she cries, I'm gonna laugh in her face."

Darian set his pen down a little harder than necessary and folded his arms. "Got nothin' to arrest her for. Guess you're outta luck."

"She broke into my house."

"Door was open."

"Bull. I didn't leave my door unlocked. And besides, she went through my things."

Darian shrugged. "Says you. Got no proof."

Alex grabbed the pictures from the floor and slapped them back on the table. "You said she took the pictures."

"I never said she took the pictures. You *assumed* she took the pictures."

"I recognize those ugly purple shoes. That's her. In my house. That's my livin' room she's standin' in right there." Alex pointed at the picture. "That's proof enough."

Darian sighed and looked away, obviously annoyed by the direction the interrogation was taking. "Fine." He shoved the notepad and pen toward Alex. "Write down what you wanna press charges for. Be specific. And sign your name."

He tapped his fingers with agitated impatience while Alex scribbled down the charges he wanted to bring against Holly with a smug smile on his face. Marx gritted his teeth. Darian was supposed to help protect

Holly from the charges, but his attempts were halfhearted at best.

"There you go. Did your job for ya." Alex pushed the pen and notepad back.

Darian read through the statement and made a disgusted noise. "You're the criminal, not her. I don't know what you expect me to do with this garbage."

"Whatever you gotta do to prove she did it. So why don't you run along and file that."

Darian grumbled beneath his breath as he stood and hammered a fist on the interrogation room door. Marx opened it for him and he stepped out, pulling the door shut behind him.

"I will not let you arrest Holly," Marx said, trying to keep control of his rising anger.

"Relax, Rick. Nobody's arrestin' Holly." He handed Marx the notepad. "I now have permission to do whatever's necessary to prove that she broke into his house and went through his things, which means his house is now a crime scene, and everythin' that Holly took a picture of or touched is evidence."

"And if those things are stolen . . ."

"Genius in there just gave me permission to collect evidence against him, all for the sake of revenge."

Marx had to admire Darian's manipulative skill, but he was still worried about what was going to happen with Holly. "I'm comin' with you.

31

Now

Holly threaded gold ribbon through the hole at the top of the gingerbread cookie, looped the ribbon at the top, and tied it.

"When I was a girl, we made all of our ornaments from scratch," Ms. Martha said. "We hung them on the tree on Christmas Eve, and feasted on cookies and candies Christmas mornin'."

Holly set her finished cookie on the tray. "Weren't the cookies stale by then?"

"Oh, we didn't care."

"Did you have Christmas lights?"

"Not for a long while. We were poor as the dirt we walked on, and those kinds of things were a luxury. But sometimes I'd put candles on the tree. It was beautiful. Until the tree caught fire. Mama gave me a good swat on the rear for that one. Didn't stop me though. I did it again the next year."

Holly laughed.

"Eventually we got lights, but I think it was 'cause Mama was tired of me settin' the tree on fire."

"We had white lights on our tree growing up," Holly said, threading another cookie. "Mom didn't like all the colors mixed together. And then we hung the ornaments. Gin and I . . ." she trailed off as the memory of her sister dredged up a storm of emotions. "Um, we weren't allowed to hang the glass ornaments because we weren't the most coordinated, and we broke a lot of them, so we got to put up the candy canes and tinsel. And Dad always picked Gin up so she could put the angel on top of the tree."

Ms. Martha smiled. "Ritchie said you two was twins. You must miss her somethin' terrible."

Holly tried to focus her attention on her gingerbread cookie. "Sometimes I wonder why I survived and she didn't. But then I think about all the awful things that happened after that, and I'm grateful that she didn't have to go through them."

Gin had been so innocent and sweet, and the foster care system would've destroyed her spirit.

Ms. Martha stretched her arm across the table and wrapped her fingers around Holly's. "Now, you listen to me, little miss Holly. I know you wish your sister had survived, but you are a precious gift to my baby and to me, and we are all so thankful that you survived, and that you're here."

Plenty of people in Holly's life had pretended to care, people she had lived with or worked with for months, but there was nothing less than genuine love in Ms. Martha's eyes.

It was overwhelming, being surrounded by so much love, and Holly looked away before it brought her to tears. "I wish I could've saved more of your ornaments."

"Don't you worry about that. We'll fill up that tree nice. Now, get your scrawny behind over there and grab that popcorn while I find some needle and fishin' line."

Holly hopped up to fetch the bowl of buttery deliciousness from in front of the microwave. She popped a few pieces in her mouth. Popcorn was amazing. She wasn't sure how much would be left for the garland once she was finished nibbling on it.

Ms. Martha paused beside Mr. Gus, who was staring out through the screen door. "What's goin' on over there?"

"Richard and Darian are over there with some officers," Mr. Gus replied.

They were searching Alex's house? Holly shuffled down the hallway with the bowl of popcorn and stretched onto her tiptoes to see over their shoulders, but decided it would be easier to look through the living room window.

She climbed onto Mr. Gus's chair and peered out the window over the back of it. She was tempted to go next door and poke around, but Marx would march her right back over here.

Camera's flashed behind the curtains, and uniformed personnel walked the premises.

"All right. Let's get started on that garland." Ms. Martha sat down on the couch with a spool of fishing line and two needles. She patted the cushion next to her. "Come on, baby."

Holly reluctantly dragged her attention from the window and plopped down beside Ms. Martha, popping another handful of popcorn into her mouth.

"You keep eatin' the decorations, we ain't gonna have nothin' left." She handed Holly one end of the thread with a needle attached. "Now be gentle."

Ms. Martha threaded her needle through a fluffy piece of popcorn and pushed it down to the center of the shared thread. Holly tried the same on her end, but her popcorn crumbled.

Ms. Martha's chest shook with laughter. "Glarin' at it ain't gonna fix it, baby. Try another."

The next few fell apart too, but by the sixth one, Holly figured out that she needed to push the needle through the center instead of the soft edges.

"I meant to thank you, Holly. For findin' my ring." The small diamond on her pinky finger sparkled in the fire light. "It was my mama's first weddin' ring. Daddy died shortly after I was born—pneumonia—and when she got remarried, she put it away in a box for me. It's nice to wear it again, but I s'pose I better put it back in the box, keep it safe until the day I find somebody to pass it down to."

Holly fetched the music box from the mantel and opened it for her. She smiled at the trace of flour on the crushed velvet. Ms. Martha was always covered in flour. Once the ring was safely back inside the box, Holly closed it and returned it to the mantel.

"You think you'll ever find a man worth marryin'?" Ms. Martha asked.

Holly fixed her attention on the popcorn garland and shook her head, hoping Ms. Martha wouldn't press any further. How could she explain that the mere idea of marrying a man was terrifying? The things that were expected of wives—she just couldn't. She *wouldn't.*

"Oh, come on now. There must be somebody who's caught your eye at one time or another."

Holly debated whether or not to answer. "There is a boy I sort of like, but we're just . . . friends." She doubted anything romantic could ever exist between them.

"Is he handsome?"

Holly's cheeks warmed and she looked away. "Maybe a little."

"A little?"

She bit her bottom lip and smiled. "Okay, very. He's very handsome. And funny and sweet. And he makes really good pizza."

"A man who cooks? You best snatch him up before somebody else does."

Sadness crept across the smile on Holly's lips. Jordan deserved someone else. Not her, not someone who was as irreparably damaged as the ornaments she'd thrown away. "He deserves someone whole and beautiful, someone who can love him in every way that he deserves."

Ms. Martha placed a hand over hers and Holly looked up, the compassion in the older woman's eyes bringing tears to hers. "Any man who truly loves you will understand, and he'll be patient and gentle with you."

The front door opened and a chilly draft swept through the house, setting the flames in the fireplace dancing. Marx's soft voice carried down the hall, "Who's ready to decorate the tree?"

32

Now

Marx held out the strand of lit white lights. "On your left."

A tiny, pale hand poked out between the branches of the tree, groping blindly at the air. He placed the coil of lights in Holly's hand and it disappeared behind the tree with her before popping out the other side.

His dad took the lights and handed them off to Marx. "You know we could manage this without her bein' behind the tree."

Marx knew their arms were long enough that they could pass the lights back and forth on their own, but Holly enjoyed helping.

"Eggnog," Mama said, handing each of them a snowflake glass too dainty for their large hands. "Holly, yours is here on the TV tray."

"I've never had eggnog." Holly leaned to see around the tree. "Is it good?"

"Mmm hmm." Marx loved Mama's homemade eggnog. No store bought carton could match it. Always too much nutmeg.

"Did you find anything else at Alex's house?" Holly asked, vanishing again. She wove the lights around the tree trunk.

"TV was in the basement and Dad's guns were in the closet." When she didn't say anything more on the subject, which was unusual for someone so curious, he asked, "What are you thinkin' that you're not sayin'?"

She squeezed out from behind the tree, and her foot snagged on the tree skirt. Marx caught her before she could hit the floor.

She blew the hair out of her face. "Thanks. And . . . I don't remember any guns."

"We found four of 'em in one of the bedrooms. They're Dad's."

Her brow furrowed in thought as she picked up her eggnog. She took a small sip and immediately spit it back into the glass, her eyes widening. "There's cinnamon in it." Her gaze moved between the eggnog and the kitchen where Mama had gone. "I don't wanna hurt her feelings, but it's gross."

Dad laughed and Marx smiled. Taking pity on her, he gulped down the last of his and traded her glasses.

Mama bustled into the room with a tray of gingerbread cookies ready to be hung on the tree and set them on the couch. "I'll get you some more eggnog, baby." She took Holly's empty glass and swept out of the room, leaving her sputtering an objection she couldn't finish.

Holly sank onto the couch next to the cookies and frowned at Marx. "Did you know she was gonna do that?"

"Mmm hmm."

Mama returned with the eggnog and Holly plastered on a grateful smile. She set the glass on the mantel, pretending to forget about it while they decorated the tree.

They draped popcorn garland across the branches and Holly stretched on tiptoes to hang a gingerbread star on one of the upper limbs. She pinched the hook around the branch and released it. It settled perfectly in the open space, the gold ribbon glistening in the light of the fire.

"When was the last time you decorated a tree, Holly?" Mama asked.

Holly thought about it as she placed a crocheted snowflake on the tree. "I kind of decorated one when I was fifteen."

Marx reached over her head to hang a candy cane. "How can you 'kind of' decorate a tree?"

"Um, the tree was actually painted on the wall since we weren't allowed to have metal or anything sharp or breakable. And we made ornaments out of glue, glitter, cotton balls, and ribbon. And then we stuck them onto the tree branches."

Dad grunted. "Where on earth were you, a prison?"

"A psychiatric facility for kids."

He blinked, caught off guard. "Oh."

"Some of the kids thought it was a prison, but I liked it there. I had my own room and there weren't any boys allowed in the girl's hallway. There wasn't much to do, but . . . it was safe."

Mama's eyes glistened in the firelight, and Marx gave her shoulder an affectionate squeeze. He'd felt that same way when he first learned that Holly had been shuffled through twelve foster homes, and then again when she told him she didn't know when her birthday was.

It was hard not to be heartbroken for that little girl, but if he cried every time Holly shared something sad from her past, he'd shrivel up from dehydration within the hour.

He nodded to Holly, who stood with a candy cane in her hand. "Are you gonna hang that or eat it?"

Holly grinned and unwrapped the stem of the candy cane, popped it into her mouth, and grabbed a second one for the tree.

Someone knocked on the door, and Marx excused himself to answer it. Darian shivered on the porch.

"Hey, sorry to bother you durin' family time, but we got a small problem." Darian held up his phone. "This is the picture that Holly took last night while Alex Martin was in custody."

Marx studied the picture on the smartphone screen, but he saw nothing out of the ordinary.

"This one,"—Darian scrolled to the next picture— "CSU took of the same closet just ten hours later, and Alex Martin is still in custody. Notice a difference?"

The guns that belonged to Marx's dad hadn't been there last night when Holly snuck in. "Somebody else had to have put them there between the time that Holly left and CSU arrived."

"Or Holly did it."

Marx speared him with a glare. "She didn't. But I have no idea who would."

"I can't tell one way or another if Alex is guilty, but he did not put those guns there."

Marx called over his shoulder for Holly, and she shuffled down the hall toward them in her slippers. "Hey, sweet pea, did you happen to notice anybody lurkin' around Martin's house last night?"

"Not lurking, but there was a man." She wrapped her sweater tighter around herself as she thought. "I think he said his name is George, and he works at a bakery. He was there looking for his nephew Bryce, but I told him he was probably arrested with the other kids."

Darian frowned. "We didn't arrest anybody named Bryce."

"Did he tell you what bakery?" Marx asked.

"No. And he didn't tell me his last name either. But he's got dark hair and he's really big in . . . well, every direction. Oh, and he has three red dot tattoos under his left eye."

Marx and Darian exchanged an interested look, but it was Darian who spoke. "Three dots around the eye is usually a prison tattoo, which means George probably has a record. I'm gonna go see what I can find out. I'll call in the mornin', hopefully with an address."

Holly tilted her head. "What do the three dots mean?"

"My crazy life. Don't ask me why it means that or who the first person was to polka dot their face. I have no idea." He wrapped his arm around her as he closed and locked the door. "Come on, let's go put the star on the tree."

33

Now

The bakery, Crazy Cakes, was easy enough to track down once Darian was able to connect it with George Calvert—a man who spent five years behind bars for theft.

The storefront window was painted with animated cupcakes and birthday cakes, dancing under a downpour of sprinkles.

Darian strode into the family-owned shop, and Marx held the door for Holly. He tried to leave her at the house, but she snatched his keys and belted herself into the passenger's seat of his car until he caved.

She admired the brightly painted walls and tall tables, then walked over to the pastry display. "Hi, George."

The large man behind the counter looked up with a smile, but it melted away the moment he noticed Marx and Darian. "You brought the cops?"

"No. *Marx* brought *me*." She pointed to a pink frosted cupcake in the display. "Can I have that one with all the sprinkles?"

George reached into the case to pull out the pink cupcake, but his attention remained on Marx and Darian, his eyes tracking their movements. He transferred the cupcake to a plate with a plastic fork and set it on the counter. "On the house."

Holly placed a crumpled five dollar bill on the counter. "I can pay for it."

George forced a smile and smoothed out the bill. "All right."

His gaze flickered around nervously, and Marx followed his attention toward the hallway that led into the kitchen. There was a metal door with an exit sign hanging above it. George was more than nervous; he was ready to run.

George gathered Holly's change and set it on the counter in front of her. "Enjoy your cupcake."

"Thanks." She carried her treat over to a nearby table and hopped up onto the stool, swiping a fingerful of frosting off the top and popping it into her mouth.

Marx angled his body between her and the cupcake counter, just in case George had a weapon stashed behind it.

Thinking along the same lines, Darian gestured George forward with his fingers. "Why don't you come out from behind the counter, Mr. Calvert. And keep your hands visible, if you don't mind."

215

George's breathing picked up, and he glanced at the exit door again. "What's this about?"

"Just come on out."

Slowly, the big man lifted a piece of the counter and squeezed through the opening. He left the counter propped up against the cupcake display and held his hands out to his sides. "I ain't done nothin' wrong."

"You sure about that? 'Cause we got a witness who places you inside a house that's not yours."

George looked past Marx at Holly, sweat slicking his forehead. "If somebody saw me in a house that ain't mine, they probably wasn't supposed to be there, either."

"A lot of things have been stolen recently, Mr. Calvert, and just so happens a man with a record of theft lives in the same area."

George shifted his jaw. "I made a mistake once, and I did my time. I'm doin' the best I can to support my family. The legal way."

"Hard to support your family the legal way when business ain't goin' too well."

The back door at the end of the hall squealed open and Marx's hand fell to his gun. But it was just an employee coming in for his shift.

The boy, oblivious to the situation in the dining area, hung his coat on a hook next to the door and tied an apron around his waist before tapping a bell on the wall.

George's attention snapped toward the bell and the young boy with curly blond hair.

A pair of small feet hit the floor behind Marx, and he glanced back to see Holly staring at the boy with recognition. The same recognition flashed across the boy's face, and he took two steps back before turning and bolting back out the door.

"Hey!" Holly took off after him.

"Holl . . ."

She thrust open the door and disappeared into the back alleyway before Marx could even finish screaming her name. He slapped a hand on the table in frustration, then sprinted after her, leaving Darian to deal with the baker.

He pushed open the door and stepped outside, scanning every direction for Holly. He was going to give her a good, long lecture later about her reckless behavior, but he had to find her first.

"Holly!"

Somebody let out a sharp cry, and he drew his gun as he hurried toward the sound. Approaching the connecting alley, he pressed his back to the wall and peered carefully around the corner.

The blond boy was crouched against a pile of boxes that looked to have been tossed out with the trash, and Holly crouched in front of him, her body language cautious but not frightened.

"Are you okay?" she asked, and she made a series of gestures with her hands that Marx had never seen her use before.

The boy shook his head and responded with an equally unusual hand-gesture.

Holly placed her fist in the center of her chest, thumb pointing toward her chin, and moved it in a circular motion. "I'm sorry. I didn't mean to scare you."

The boy was deaf, and Holly was speaking to him in sign language. Marx put away his gun, unsure whether to be amazed or furious.

He stepped into the alley and the boy shifted, his eyes fixed on Marx's gun. Holly tried to calm him. "He's my friend." She watched the boy's response, then smiled. "Yes, he's a cop."

Marx crouched beside her, keeping his movements nonthreatening. He might not read sign language, but he read body language, and this boy didn't trust him. To Holly, he asked, "Where did you learn to speak sign language?"

"At the psychiatric facility when I was a kid. One of the girls in my group never talked to anyone, and one day I asked her why."

"She was deaf."

Holly nodded. "She'd been there for almost a year, and the only person who could understand her was her therapist. She seemed so lonely, so I asked her to teach me to sign. I'm not very good at it, but we did have some pretty funny conversations."

Marx smiled. "You never cease to amaze me. And what's this young man's name?"

Holly opened her mouth to answer, but the boy responded first, indignation sharpening his movements. When he finished, he looked at Holly to interpret. Holly squinted, seeming to struggle with it. "I'm sorry, I don't . . . that was too fast."

The boy let out a flustered breath and signed slower, doing his best to pronounce the words as he shaped them. "I'm deaf, not stupid. I can read lips. Talk to me."

It took Marx a moment to make sense of what he said, but the message was clear. He wanted to be spoken *to*, not spoken *about*. "Sorry. What's your name?"

"Bryce." To Holly, he said with a teasing smile, "Your sign is terrible. I've seen babies do better."

Holly grinned, not taking offense. "He's the boy I saw outside the kitchen window. I couldn't describe him, but when I saw him, I recognized him."

Bryce hastened to explain. "I was just looking. I'm not a . . ."

Marx couldn't make out the last word, and Holly shook her head when he looked to her to interpret. Bryce rolled his eyes, as though their ignorance was a burden on his teenage life.

He picked up a pebble and scratched three words into the blacktop—*not a creep*—then lifted his eyebrows as if to say, "do you get it now?"

"You're not a creep. Yes, I understand. But what were you lookin' for in my family's home?"

Bryce swallowed hard and looked away. Marx was certain he understood the question; he just didn't want to answer it. After a long moment, he sighed and signed, "Things to sell."

Marx tapped his hand to bring his eyes up. "Did you break into my family's home?"

Reluctantly, Bryce nodded. Holly's shoulders dropped, and she cast Marx a pained look. She already cared about the boy, and she didn't want him to go to prison.

"Why?" Marx demanded.

Bryce's expression implored them to understand. "For Uncle George. Business is bad, and we can't pay the bills. Got a foreclosure notice on the house." When neither of them understood the word foreclosure, he spelled it out one letter at a time. "Uncle George tried to get a second job, but no one will hire him because of his record. And no one will hire me because I'm deaf. I didn't know what else to do."

Marx rubbed a hand over his face. What was he supposed to do with this information? "How did my family's things end up in Alex Martin's house?"

Bryce blinked and then looked at Holly, signing something that must have been a question, because she shook her head.

"No, you didn't misunderstand. The ring and the guns were found in Alex's house. Do you know how they got there?"

Bryce shrugged, genuine confusion on his face. He wasn't the person who had moved the items to Alex's house.

"You saw his uncle there. Maybe George realized what he did and tried to get rid of the evidence."

Bryce sat straight, his hands flying a mile a minute, and Holly struggled to keep up.

"I don't . . . you have to slow down, Bryce. I don't know what you're . . ." When he repeated the same gestures, emphasizing them, Holly relayed the message. "Uncle George didn't do anything wrong. I did."

And then Bryce lost her again, launching into what Marx could only assume was a teenage rant. He ended his long speech by holding up his middle finger.

Marx grunted. "I know what that one means. Come on, kid. Let's go have a chat with your uncle."

He grabbed Bryce's arm and pulled him to his feet, walking him back into the cupcake shop with Holly just steps behind.

George, who sat at one of the tables with his wrists cuffed behind his back, sprang to his feet the moment Marx marched Bryce back into the bakery. "Let him go. He ain't done nothin'."

Marx couldn't help but notice the lack of resemblance between the two. George had Latino heritage, and Bryce was Caucasian. "He says you're his uncle."

"I *am* his uncle. I was adopted when I was seven. Dad already had a daughter, my sister Emma. Bryce is her son. He came to live with me after she died."

Darian stood beside the large man, ready to grab him if he tried to make a move. "George here says he's the one who broke into your family's house."

221

"Interestin'. That's not what Bryce told us."

"Bryce is deaf, and he don't speak much neither. So unless you can sign, I don't believe you."

"I don't have to sign." Marx threw a thumb over his shoulder at Holly. "She signs."

George's massive shoulders slumped, and he looked at his nephew with a deep sadness in his eyes. "I told you I'd take care of it. Why'd you tell them?"

Bryce signed his reply, his words slow and heavy, as though weighted by the same sadness. "You taught me to be honest."

George sank back onto the stool. "I s'pose I did." He sighed and looked at Marx. "And I guess that means I should be honest, too. I put your family's things in Alex Martin's house."

Marx had figured that much, but what he didn't know was why. "If you were afraid we'd find out Bryce was the thief, there were other ways you could've gotten rid of the evidence. You could've thrown it out or sold it. Why put it in Alex's house?"

"I told you I made a mistake a long time ago, but I ain't that man no more. I wanted your family to have their things back. Ain't like I could just walk up to the door and hand 'em over, though. After Alex was arrested, I figured nobody would be there that night, so I moved everythin' over. I thought it'd be the safest and quickest way to get your things back to your family." He tipped his head toward Holly. "I wasn't expectin' her to show up in the middle."

Holly scrunched her face apologetically. "Oops."

"Alex is always stealin' stuff. Bryce seen some of the things he stole before I made him stop goin' over there. He's the one who told me where to find Alex's stash of jewelry, 'cause he seen him stuffin' it in the sink one day."

Darian looked mildly annoyed. "The problem, Mr. Calvert, is that even if Alex Martin stole from every person in the neighborhood, *you* planted stolen property in his house. That gives him a rock solid defense."

"I'm sorry, but I wasn't thinkin' about that. All I was thinkin' about is my nephew. I'll do whatever you want me to do. I'll testify against Martin if you want. But please, officers, Bryce don't deserve to go to prison."

Marx didn't envy the mess that Darian was going to have to sort through. He would do his best to convince his parents not to press charges against Bryce, but beyond that, there was nothing he could do to help either of them.

34

Now

The fire crackled and the flames cast dancing shadows along the walls, filling his family's living room with life.

Neatly wrapped packages were arranged around The Nativity beneath the tree, some finished off with ribbons and bows, while others—Marx's mainly—were so ugly and deformed that they were hidden in the back.

He sat on the sofa, admiring the tree decorated with the simplest of things. The lights warmed the popcorn garland, and the entire room smelled like family movie night with popcorn and cinnamon candy.

Holly had even sacrificed a few s'more-sized marshmallows to make snowman ornaments. But he doubted those would make it beyond the first fifteen minutes of Christmas morning. She was already nibbling on one as she leaned against him on the couch.

She smiled up at him, her face glowing with joy, and he kissed her forehead.

Thank you, Lord, for that smile.

All he had hoped for by bringing her here was this moment, this glow of happiness radiating from her. Christmas with family was something so many took for granted, but it truly was a gift, and even though half the packages under the tree were for Holly, he knew that spending Christmas with his family would be the most precious gift of all.

She offered him the head of the marshmallow snowman on a toothpick. "Want some?"

He snorted in amusement. "You're obsessed with marshmallows." He looked across the living room at Mama, who was wrapping up one last gift.

"Would you hold your finger still?" she snapped at Dad, trying to tie a ribbon around his finger.

"I am holdin' still," Dad snapped back. "But you could be a bit quicker. Rapture's gonna come before you finish with that ribbon."

Marx never thought he would spend another Christmas with his family, let alone enjoy one. But there was a sense of peace in his heart as he watched his parents.

Holly was right. Holding on to all that pain and bitterness toward his father had been robbing him of that peace, weighing so heavily on his heart over the past thirty years that it was a wonder he didn't smother.

There was only one thing that would make this Christmas complete: Cressy, his big sister.

Mama placed the last gift under the tree. "All right. Let's open presents!"

"Wait!" Holly sprung off the couch and grabbed her camera. "I have to take pictures."

Marx's phone vibrated, and he grabbed it off the mantel. There was a message from Darian.

One of the kids rolled and said that Martin has been enticing them to steal for him, so Martin is on the hook for multiple robberies, but he agreed to drop the B&E charges against Holly if we drop the assault and battery charges against him.

Marx replied with a quick message before closing his phone and setting it aside.

Thanks for the update. Merry Christmas.

Holly plopped back down with her camera and a gift. "Now we can open presents." She handed it to Marx.

"Holly, you know I don't want you spendin' your money on me."

"You spend money on me all the time."

"Yes, but that's different."

"Why?"

"Because . . ." He tried to think up a good reason that wouldn't earn him an indignant glare, but nothing came to mind. "Because it just is."

She rolled her eyes. "Just open your present."

He smiled at the nametag addressed to Sugar, then ripped off the green wrapping paper and opened the box. There was a picture frame inside with a photo of the two of them together. He didn't remember it being taken or who had taken it, but there it was.

Engraved into the bottom of the frame was a saying:

We may not share a name,
And our blood may not be the same,
But love is not defined by words,
And the truth of the heart will always be heard.

-To the dad of my heart, love Holly.

The letters blurred through his tears, and Marx pulled Holly into a tight hug. "I love you too, baby."

"Well let's see it," Mama urged, and Marx pulled the picture frame from the box and held it up for his parents to see.

As he looked at it, he realized there was something off about it. He tipped his head to make sure it wasn't just the angle messing with his perception, and Holly snickered. "This picture frame is crooked. Intentionally."

Holly's snicker dissolved into a full-on mischievous giggle. It wasn't bad enough that she tilted the pictures on his apartment wall, now she found one that he couldn't possibly straighten no matter how hard he tried.

"You are nothin' but mischief, you know that?"

She covered her mouth with a hand, but a squeaking snort escaped, sending ripples of laughter around the room.

They exchanged the rest of the gifts. Mama got a new apron from Holly, and Dad got slippers. Mama made Marx a box full of fattening sweets for the trip home and bought him a camouflage coffee mug.

Holly opened her gifts with agonizing slowness, preserving the paper like it might be the last Christmas wrap ever made.

The expression on her face when she unwrapped her Easy Bake Oven was priceless: excitement, confusion, swiftly followed by suspicion. "Does this mean I'm not allowed to use your oven anymore?"

"Now you can bake in your bedroom and quit settin' off my smoke alarms."

She grinned. "There's a smoke alarm in there, too."

Her next gift was a Keurig coffee maker. Or rather, it was a gift for Marx so she stopped butchering his coffee in the morning. But he made sure to include a container of mini marshmallows and half a dozen hot chocolate pods to put into the dispenser.

"Heads-up." Marx tossed a soft package over Holly's head to Mama.

Mama fumbled to catch it. "Richard Damascus! You do not throw things in the house!"

Holly's mouth dropped open and she turned her head slowly to gape at him. "Damascus?"

"Mama!"

Mama waved off his complaint. "Don't you Mama me. You broke the rules, and that's what that middle name is for."

Holly grinned. "Richard Damascus Marx. That's gonna come in handy."

"Hush." He plopped his hand over her face and pushed her over into the pillows.

Dad stood and carried a small gift box over, handing it to Marx. Marx accepted it with cautious curiosity—Dad was not a gift giver. He pulled the lid off the box to find a key resting inside.

"This is the key to your old truck."

"I thought maybe it was time to . . . let it go."

The meaning behind his dad's words went far deeper than simply handing over a set of keys. He was letting go of the past.

Marx closed his hands over the truck keys. "I think it's time to let it go, too."

A mysterious shine filled Dad's eyes, and he looked away as he cleared his throat. "Good. And if you feel like fixin' it up, and you might possibly want a hand with that, well . . . there's sure to be a few years before I'm dead, so . . . I'll be here."

That might have been the nicest thing his dad had ever said to him.

"And there's, uh . . . a Winchester rifle in the truck bed. You can do whatever you want with it. Just . . . take it."

The gun that had been used to take his grandfather's life. He wasn't sure he wanted it any more than Dad did, but maybe he could find somebody who would do something good with it. "I'll find a place for it to go."

Dad nodded and headed over to his recliner. Mama had one last gift for Holly, and Marx leaned forward with interest. He didn't know about this one.

"This one's for you, baby."

Holly took the tiny box from Mama's hand and opened it, her face becoming curiously blank as she stared at the contents. Finally she closed the lid and looked up. "Ms. Martha, I can't take this."

"You most certainly can."

"But you're saving it for—"

"For my grandbaby." Mama reached over and squeezed Holly's hand.

Tears glistened on Holly's cheeks and she reopened the box to study Mama's diamond ring. She seemed to struggle with the idea that she was now part of his family, that his mama claimed her as a grandbaby. "But . . . I'm never gonna get married."

"Yes, you will, baby." Mama smiled through her own tears. "The Good Lord's gonna keep on healin' you, and one day you'll be ready to take that step, to entrust your heart . . . and your body . . . to a man who will cherish you like the precious gift that you are."

Holly wrapped her arms around Mama's neck and hugged her. "Thank you."

Mama smiled at Marx as she rubbed Holly's back. "You're so welcome, honey."

The doorbell rang.

"I'll get it." Marx pushed himself off the couch and checked through the window beside the door to see who was there, hoping it wasn't Darian, and then quickly opened the door.

Standing on the porch was a woman who could've been his twin. A woman he hadn't seen in years. "Cresceda!"

"Hi, baby brother." She limped forward to give him a hug, and he squeezed her tight. "It's so good to see you." She pulled back and held out a container of cupcakes with a card stuck to the top addressed to: *Officer Marx.* "These were sittin' on the porch."

Curious, Marx took the card and opened it. It was from George and Bryce, wishing his family a Merry Christmas, and thanking them for not pressing charges. Mama had agreed to drop the charges in a heartbeat, but Dad had taken a little convincing.

There was a folded slip of paper inside the card with a handwritten note on it.

I added this at the last second so Bryce wouldn't know. He don't have many friends 'cause of his condition. But he took a liking to Holly. She was kind to him, and I think it would do him good to have a friend. If she don't mind keeping in touch, here's his email and text number. Thank her for me and tell her to enjoy the extra sprinkles on the cupcakes.

-George.

Marx smiled and closed the card. Holly would certainly appreciate the sprinkles.

Cressy pinched at the silver hair around his temples. "Look at you, turnin' gray."

"There's a reason for that, and her name is Holly."

Not that Cressy had any business commenting on *his* gray hair. She was three years older, and the only reason she didn't have any visible gray was because she dyed it.

Cressy gasped. "Mama told me about her. Is she here? I wanna meet her." She didn't wait for an answer before bustling into the house.

Marx closed the door and walked back into the living room. His family was all in one place. Happy, healthy, and overflowing with love.

This was Christmas.

EPILOGUE

A little sleigh bell jingled above the door as Holly stepped into JGH Investigations, and she looked up at it with a smile.

She loved spending Christmas with Marx's family, but it was nice to be back in New York City. She looked around the office as she walked to the reception counter.

A snowman mug of candy canes sat next to a red-and-white striped mug of mint marshmallows. A tag hung from the handle of the marshmallow mug. Did Jordan forget to remove the price tag? She lifted it to get a closer look.

Grab some marshmallows and check out the tree.

Curious, she snagged a couple marshmallows and walked over to the Christmas tree Jordan had put up.

It was real.

She ran her fingers over the branches, admiring the twinkling lights and red and silver bows. A clear ornament hanging from a silver chain drew her eye, and a skinny slip of paper enclosed inside read: *take the ornament and check the office.*

She grinned, enjoying the cute little game Jordan had created, and took the ornament with her. She opened the door to her office, an oblong room with eggplant purple walls and packed bookshelves.

Turning in a slow circle, she searched for the next clue. She laughed when she found it hanging from the ceiling. He would put it all the way up there.

She grabbed her step stool and stretched onto her tiptoes, grabbing a hold of the clear ornament and pulling free. She sank back to her heels and examined her little clue. There were silver charms inside the ornament, and another note: *Don't forget to let the dog out.*

She puzzled over the peculiar message as she climbed off her stool. Where was Riley anyway?

His dog pillow was empty. She carried around her clue as she scanned the office for her German shepherd. "Riley?"

One of the other office doors opened and Riley squeezed out, barking and whining with excitement as he barreled toward her.

She sank to her knees and hugged her fuzzy companion around the neck. "Oh, I missed you."

She released his neck and pulled back, laughing when he tried to lick her face from chin to forehead.

"What's this?" A small gift box dangled from Riley's collar. She untied it and opened it, drawing in a breath of amazement.

A silver, oval pendant with her initials engraved on it rested on a bed of white cotton. Gently, she removed the pendant, and her finger brushed along a tiny hinge.

It was a locket.

She opened it to find a small picture of her and Jordan as children on one side, and one of her family on the other. It was a different picture than the one she had—different and yet so beautiful. Now she had two.

A trembling breath escaped her and she wiped at her eyes with the sleeve of her shirt.

"My mom spoke to pretty much everyone in town until she found someone with a picture of your family." Jordan's voice was soft when he spoke, and she looked up to see him leaning in the doorway of the room Riley had come out of. "I wanted you to have a picture of your family to take with you wherever you go."

"Thank you." It wasn't enough, but those were the only words she could find right now.

He crouched beside her, his nearness sending a flutter through her stomach that wasn't caused by fear. He collected the silver chain and charms from the first few clues, and pieced the necklace together.

"Can I help you put it on?"

She hesitated briefly, but then pulled her hair aside. Her instincts warned her not to let a man put his hands near her neck, but she ignored them, even as his fingertips grazed the back of her neck and sent a shiver down her spine.

"There we go." He released the chain and the locket fell to rest over her ribs.

She couldn't stop staring at it. It was stunning, and the picture of her family inside . . . it was so precious. She met Jordan's blue eyes. "Thank you so much." She paused before adding apologetically, "I didn't know what to get you."

"Good. That means I get to pick my present."

The impish smile that quirked his lips made her wary. "Maybe, depending on what you want."

"The whole day."

"What do you mean?"

"I wanna spend the rest of the day together, watching Christmas movies, eating popcorn, making Jolly sundaes with extra sprinkles. Oh, and I wanna hear about Georgia." He rose and waited for her to do the same. When she didn't, the excitement in his eyes dimmed. "Unless you don't wanna do that."

"Oh, I do. I'm just waiting for you to offer me a hand up."

He blinked. "You never want a hand up."

He was right. She almost never accepted help to her feet. She was capable of doing it on her own, but she wanted an excuse to touch him, to feel his warm skin against hers again. Just briefly.

Jordan bowed gallantly and offered his hand. "My lady. When you're ready."

She slipped her hand into his slowly, their fingertips brushing softly against each other. It was unsettling and pleasant at the same time, and she forced her mind to focus solely on the pleasant part.

He lifted her to her feet and their hands remained connected a second longer than necessary before she let go and stepped back. She smiled, her face hot, and her belly fluttering.

This was definitely going to be the best Christmas she'd had in a very long time.

C.C. Warrens

THE END

How to Connect

Facebook: https://www.facebook.com/ccwarrens
Website: https://www.ccwarrensbooks.com/
Email: ccwarrens@yahoo.com

For previous books in the series, check out Injustice for All.

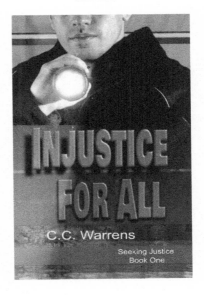

Made in the USA
Coppell, TX
05 October 2020